For Bella, my shadow of fourteen years.

BRONZE

Elise Noble

Published by Undercover Publishing Limited

Copyright © 2019 Elise Noble

v6

ISBN: 978-1-912888-10-8

Edited by Amanda Ann Larson

Cover design by Abigail Sins

www.undercover-publishing.com

www.elise-noble.com

CHAPTER 1 - KYLIE

"WELCOME BACK TO Australia, Mrs. Watson. Enjoy your trip."

The immigration officer handed back my passport, and I fought to maintain the slightly aloof expression I'd been practising in front of the mirror for the past week, when what I really wanted to do was cry with relief.

Relief that I hadn't been arrested on sight.

My heart hammered in my chest as "Mr. Watson" cleared passport control behind me then placed a hand on the small of my back to steer me out to the waiting limo. A freaking limo. How the other half lived.

The driver took my fancy leather luggage—monogrammed with my fake initials, KW, which was a nice touch—and it was only then that I noticed my hands were shaking, a definite tremble I tried to hide by shoving them into my pockets. Then I realised I didn't have any pockets because I was wearing a designer dress that probably cost more than the monthly salary I used to earn as a police officer.

Back in those days, I never used to tremble.

"Good flight, ma'am?" the driver asked as I slid into the car.

"Very good, thank you."

The driver wasn't in on the secret. As far as the staff

at the Black Diamond Hotel and Spa were concerned, I was just another rich bitch flying in for a quiet but luxurious holiday on the Queensland coast, a week or two of R & R at the secluded resort an hour or so north of Brisbane.

"There's chilled champagne in the cooler. Traffic's light, so we should have a smooth ride. If you'd like to order dinner ahead of your arrival, I can call through to the chef."

"I'm not hungry," I said, then remembered my manners. "Russell? How about you?"

"Huh?"

He glanced up from his phone, where his nose had been buried for half of the flight from the US. For the other half, he'd been engrossed in his laptop.

"Do you want to order dinner?"

"Uh, right, I'm fine with whatever."

So, that'd be one plate of nothing and one plate of anything, then.

"Could you just ask the chef to send some snacks?" I said to the driver.

"Of course, ma'am."

Bodybuilder butterflies pounded my stomach, trying to batter their way out. Every time we rounded a bend, I looked for the police cruiser, waited for the siren, the flashing lights. The ink on my arrest warrant might have been dry, but the cops would never forget, especially since the person who'd framed me for murder was one of their own.

My ex-boss to be precise, who also happened to be my ex-boyfriend. Detective Sergeant Michael Brenner of the Brisbane City Tactical Crime Squad.

Every so often while I was on the run, I'd looked

him up on the internet out of morbid curiosity. Had his deception been discovered yet? No, it hadn't. Not only was he still in his job, he'd received a bloody medal late last year after saving a child from a burning building.

If I had to guess, I'd say he probably lit the fire himself. That was the kind of dirtbag he was.

Outside the car, everything was green. So much green. Such a difference from Egypt, where I'd been living until recently. I had to stop myself from pressing my nose to the window, from rolling the glass down to inhale the sweet, rain-soaked air as eucalyptus trees rustled above us in the breeze.

I'd grown up not too far from there in Rocky Ridge, a little town famous for having the best ice cream parlour in Queensland. The Ice House served over a hundred flavours, which was somewhat dangerous since the wait staff wore roller skates. But they'd had a lot of practice, and I'd never once seen them drop anything.

Back when I was free, I'd spent every holiday driving up and down this road, visiting the tourist attractions along the way, usually with my best friend, Chloe, sitting beside me rather than a half-stranger I was pretending to be married too. In those days, I'd dreamed of travelling the world, of seeing the exotic places from the TV in person, but once I left, all I wanted was to be back home.

Where was Chloe now? I'd sent one last email to her before I left town, explaining the situation, saying I was sorry and begging her not to believe the lies, but I hadn't been in contact since. Did she hate me? I couldn't blame her if she did. I'd missed her freaking wedding. For all I knew, she had a child now. Two children. Three. A family.

And speaking of family, I'd abandoned them too. My parents still lived in Rocky Ridge, in the house where I'd grown up, a compact white bungalow on a small plot just five minutes' walk from The Ice House. Dad used to keep chickens in the yard. Did he still have chickens?

Would I ever find out?

I'd spent the past three years thinking I'd never set foot in my home country again. Three years when I'd travelled from Honduras to Russia to Costa Rica to Cape Verde to Tunisia to Algeria to Egypt, none of it through choice, heading anywhere without an extradition treaty with Australia. I thought I'd have to keep running forever, until one day in Egypt, I got two new neighbours whose arrival set off a chain of events that left over twenty people dead and me on a private jet fleeing yet another country. The same jet I'd just stepped off, in fact.

Russell has been in Egypt too, and for better or for worse, he'd volunteered to pose as my husband for this trip. The police would be looking for a fugitive travelling alone, not a happily married woman with an admittedly handsome spouse.

Russell hadn't offered his services out of altruism, though. No, he'd offered them out of guilt. Guilt that an app he'd designed had played a part in both the trouble in Egypt and the shambles my life had become. This was his way of lightening the load, and I had no choice but to accept his help.

And I could have done worse, I suppose. From what I'd seen of Russell, he had two sides. The charming, gentlemanly side—the man who opened doors and offered you his seat and always said please and thank you. Then there was the workaholic side. Once he got his head down in front of his laptop, nothing short of a nuclear blast would distract him from his task. To him, computer programming wasn't so much a job as an obsession. But like I said, it could have been worse. At least he wouldn't hurt me the way Michael did, and he'd top up my wine at dinner.

But if Russell was my sidekick, the heavy lifting had been done by Emmy Black, a new acquaintance I'd met in Egypt. I had to call her an acquaintance because she didn't strike me as the kind of woman who made friends easily. She part-owned the jet, and the Black Diamond Resort, and Blackwood Security, whose services she'd offered to fix my mess. Or at least, attempt to fix it. Personally. I couldn't see a way out of the predicament, but I also couldn't afford to pass up the opportunity to try.

Her parting gift to me had been a new passport in the name of Kyanna Watson. For the last three years, I'd been Tegan Wallace, and while I wasn't yet able to call myself Kylie Nichols again, I was one step closer with the Ky part.

The car turned down a driveway and purred past a sign welcoming us to the Black Diamond. We meandered under spreading poinciana trees and lollipop-shaped tuckeroos lit up by strategically placed lights, their foliage reminding me again of the garden at home. Dad had loved his garden, and by the age of six, I'd been able to name every plant and tree in it. I gave in and opened the window, and the scent of frangipani drifted in. I'd missed my home so, so much.

The main lodge came into view, a single-storey

building that sprawled in front of us. I knew from Emmy's briefing that it contained a breakfast room, restaurant, spa, library, gym, and conference rooms. Accommodation was in luxury villas tucked away amongst the trees on the twenty-hectare estate. Russell and I would be staying in Emmy's own villa, a three-bedroom affair just a stone's throw from the beach. In separate bedrooms, of course.

Before the driver could get my door, a smaller man hurried out of the lodge and tugged it open.

"Mr. and Mrs. Watson? Welcome to the Black Diamond. I'm Akeem, your concierge for this evening."

He beamed at us, waving a porter over as he stepped back to let us exit. Russell went first, holding out a hand for me. You'd think he'd been working undercover his whole life when in actual fact, that had been my job.

We followed Akeem inside, and he didn't stop talking the whole way.

"So, you'll be staying in Emmy and Black's private villa. The master bedroom's off-limits, but we've opened up everything else for you. Bradley called ahead and asked me to stock up on groceries for you in case you want to cook"—Bradley was Emmy's assistant —"although of course we can deliver room service twenty-four-seven and the restaurant's right through there." He waved a hand to his left. "We've made tea for you. Would you like it here or at the villa?"

"I'm more of a coffee drinker," Russell told him.

I couldn't help giggling. "He means dinner."

"Oh. Do people drink tea here?"

"Of course they do. It's even grown here. Just ask for a cuppa if you want one."

"I wouldn't mind a glass of wine. And we'll eat in the villa if it's not too much trouble."

Akeem clapped his hands together. "No trouble at all. Red, white, or rosé?"

I snorted a little at the idea of Russell drinking rosé, but he gave a polite smile.

"Red, please."

"If you could just sign in, I'll show you to the villa. George," he called to the porter. "Take the luggage to villa 666."

Six-six-six? Well, that was appropriate considering who it belonged to.

Named after the devil or not, the villa was beautiful. Each spacious double bedroom had its own bathroom complete with a giant tub, a walk-in shower, and a collection of toiletries in a basket by the sink. In the living room, three sofas clustered around an entertainment area on one side, next to an open-plan kitchen and dining area. Beyond, folding glass doors opened up to a terrace that came with half a dozen sun loungers and our own pool, all surrounded by palm trees, jacarandas, and a whole collection of tropical plants.

Under any other circumstances, I'd have been in heaven at the thought of spending a week or two there, but with things as they were, I couldn't tamp down the gnawing feeling of apprehension.

"Can I book you any spa treatments? Arrange some excursions?" Akeem offered. "We have our own boat if you want to go scuba diving or snorkelling."

I shook my head, then regretted aggravating my fledgling headache. "No, thank you. We already have plans for tomorrow. Did our hire car get delivered?"

Bradley had promised to arrange transport too.

"A hire car? No, no. He said you'd be using Emmy's car. The keys are in the nightstand in the pink bedroom along with some other goodies." He gave me a wink I wasn't sure I liked. "The car's parked in the carport at the side. Just turn right out of the lobby. Toodles."

He backed out the door, closing it behind him with a quiet click.

"Goodies? What's that supposed to mean?" Russell asked.

"Let's take a look, shall we?"

I found the car key nestled in a pile of condoms of every conceivable colour, flavour, and texture. There were also three kinds of lube, a pair of handcuffs, and some toys I had no idea what to do with.

"Safe to say they've got completely the wrong idea about why we're here."

"Which is a good thing, yes?" Russell picked out a pink ostrich feather. "Not really my colour."

I was more interested in the key. The little black fob had a silver pony running across the back of it.

"Holy shit. Emmy's lent us a Mustang?"

"Is that good or bad? My type of car comes with a chauffeur."

"Are you serious?"

"I live in London. If I need to go somewhere, I take the Tube or hire a town car."

"I meant, you seriously don't know what a Mustang is? Don't you have a driver's licence?"

I did, courtesy of Emmy. And a birth certificate and an Australian Medicare card too. She didn't do things by halves. I just hoped I wouldn't need to use Medicare when this was over.

"I learned to drive a decade ago, but I've never owned a vehicle. What's the point? In London, I'd spend most of my time sitting in traffic."

"Looks like I'll be doing the driving, then." Although in a Mustang, I couldn't say I minded.

"Leyton's coming here tomorrow, isn't he?"

"Yes, at nine."

Leyton was Leyton Rix, a senior investigator from Blackwood's Brisbane office. He'd been assigned to help with my case, and boy did I feel sorry for the guy. I'd spoken to him on the phone last week, and he sounded far more positive than I felt. But we were asking him to do the impossible. Firstly, we had to prove my innocence in a case where the evidence was stacked against me, and secondly, we needed to get Michael put in jail where he belonged. And the Queensland Police Service's shining star wouldn't go quietly, of that I was sure.

Chapter 2 - Kylie

THE NEXT MORNING, Russell was already sitting at the dining table when I got up, complete with two laptops and a carafe of coffee. When he saw me, he poured life-giving caffeine into an empty cup and held it out.

"You look as though you need this."

I was too tired to be insulted. "Thanks."

"Didn't sleep well?"

"Every time I heard a noise outside, I thought someone was coming to arrest me."

"They won't. Not at the moment, anyway. Your case is more or less cold. Nobody spotted you at the airport, so they're not going to suddenly turn up and break the door down."

"You don't know that for sure."

"I do, actually." Before I could ask how, he gestured towards the laptops in front of him. "What do you think I've been doing for the last month?"

"I hadn't really thought about it."

When we left Egypt, he'd flown to Virginia with the rest of us—me, Emmy, her colleague Logan, plus Tai and Ren, my former neighbours, and Ren's boss Jed. But while everyone else had stayed in Virginia, Russell had flown back to London after two weeks, citing work commitments. I'd been too stressed to speak to him much at Riverley, Emmy's home in the US, and I hadn't seen him again until the day before yesterday. Yes, I probably should have paid more attention to him, but he was only meant to be a decoy, not an operational member of the team.

When I first met him, I'd assumed he was just another city boy, one of the dime-a-dozen suited clones that inhabited every business district from Brisbane to Brussels, but it turned out he was a hacker. White-hat by day, and—I suspected—black-hat by night. Seemed he'd just confirmed that.

"You got into the QPS's network?"

"They really should update their anti-virus software. One of the little fishes took the bait a week ago."

"Which fish? Do you know?"

"Arlo Clarke."

"Superintendent Clarke? Oh my goodness. He was my supervisor. And he used to make us take this stupid cybersecurity test every three months, one with fake emails and cartoon fish, and if we were a day late, he'd threaten to put us on desk duty until we caught up."

"Perhaps he should've practised what he preached."

"What did you send him? Tell me it was a link to a porn site?"

The corner of Russell's lip twitched. "Sorry to disappoint. It was a discount voucher for Domino's pizza. No one can resist seventy-five percent off. I'm still going through his data, but there's been no traffic mentioning your name in the last twenty-four hours. If someone had an inkling you were in the country, they'd most likely have contacted Clarke."

Russell was right; they would. Which meant my

stomach could stop flipping long enough for me to eat something.

"Clarke always did like his food. And speaking of food…"

"Breakfast will be here any…" A knock sounded. "Minute."

I took a step towards the door, then hesitated as an irrational fear took hold. The logical part of me knew it was only room service. But my inner conspiracy theorist saw Michael or Owen or Shane, the three people I was sure were mixed up in all this.

"Want me to get it?" Russell offered. He was surprisingly perceptive when he took his face out of his computer.

"No, it's fine."

I forced myself to walk. To reach out, unlock the door, and turn the handle. And yes, it was only a waiter with a cart, and how many bloody dishes had Russell ordered?

One of everything, it seemed, and he remembered to thank the waiter too.

"I hope half of this is for you," I said once the waiter closed the door.

"No, I rarely eat breakfast."

My eyes rolled all of their own accord. "Then why did you order so much?"

"I wasn't sure what you'd want, so I asked them to bring a selection. I'm sure Leyton'll help you to finish it if you're not that hungry. He's on his way."

"How do you know? Are you tracking his phone?"

"His assistant called to tell me."

Oh.

Fortunately, when Leyton turned up ten minutes

later, he'd brought a friend, a petite brunette he introduced as Mimi Tran, also with Blackwood. She didn't look like a native—coupled with her surname, I guessed she had some Vietnamese blood in her. Her age? I had no idea. She had one of those faces that could have been anywhere from eighteen to thirty-five. An undercover officer's dream. Put her in a school uniform, and she'd pass for a student. Give her a business suit, and she'd be equally at home in a boardroom. She came with a fat notepad and a serious expression, but at least she took a danish.

Leyton was younger than I expected—in his early thirties at a guess, with dark brown hair and dark eyes at odds with his bright smile. Those teeth could have launched their own toothpaste range. I half expected a cartoon twinkle and a *ping* every time he opened his mouth.

"I got the basics from Emmy, but it always helps to hear a client tell the story in their own words," he said. "Would you mind?"

I hated talking about that time. Hated to even think about it, but I nodded anyway.

"It started exactly a week after my twenty-third birthday. I remember because the previous Thursday, I was sitting in a Chinese restaurant with Michael and the rest of my friends, eating crispy wontons until I was stuffed. Do you know what my fortune cookie said? *Your high-minded principles spell success.* Which turned out to be utter bullshit. Sorry, I shouldn't swear."

"Go right ahead. I'm used to it from Mimi."

Really? Mimi looked too sweet to curse. Like a china doll, pale apart from a deep red slash of lipstick.

"Anyhow, that Thursday, I was supposed to meet a CI. A covert informant."

He nodded because of course he knew what a CI was. It was me who was stupid. Still, Russell looked as if he appreciated the explanation, which made me feel a little better.

"I'd been a cop for five years at that point. It was all I'd ever wanted to do, and I joined the QPS right after my eighteenth birthday. I was still a constable when everything fell apart, but I'd got my dream transfer a year previously, to Task Force Titan in the Tactical Crime Squad. Michael ran it, and his solve rate was second to none. Still is, probably, because he doesn't play by the rules."

"In what way?"

"This is all hindsight, and I don't have any definitive proof, but I'm ninety-nine percent certain I'm right."

"Tell us what you think."

"I think he accepted bribes from a group of drug dealers."

"To look the other way?"

"And also to take out the competition. They gave him the information to do so, and that's why he made so many busts. All the little things make sense now—the way he dismissed some tips and acted on others, how evidence dropped into his lap, the extra money he always seemed to have. He had a boat, did you know that? He told everyone he bought it with a life insurance settlement from his dad, but I don't think his dad's even dead. I'm sure I heard them talking on the phone once."

Leyton nodded, and Mimi took notes in neat

handwriting. She still hadn't said a word, other than a thank-you for the pastry.

"We can check into that. Any idea where his family live?"

"He grew up in Cairns, but he never talked much about his childhood. He told me his mum died of cancer when he was a teenager, but I'm not certain that's true either."

"Brothers? Sisters?"

"He never mentioned any. This sounds awful, doesn't it? That I dated the man for seven months and barely knew him."

"It happens. Last month, we had a case where a wife wanted to know why her husband of eight years came home smelling of perfume once or twice. Turned out he had a whole other family. A kid and everything. She was a smart lady, a doctor, but he was a good liar."

"And Michael was a police officer," Russell said. "They're supposed to be trustworthy."

It was sweet of them to try and make me feel better, but I still wanted to kick myself. I'd hoped to be a detective, for crying out loud, and I'd missed the snake slithering right under my own nose.

"Well, they're not. They set me up. As I said, I was supposed to be meeting a CI, but he didn't show. I figured he'd just got cold feet, but he was dead. They killed him in his house and made it look like I did it."

"They?"

"Michael and his buddies."

"What were you meant to meet the CI about?" Leyton asked. "And where?"

"The usual place—a park near his home—but I don't know what about. He just called me and said he had some information I needed to hear."

"Is that normal?" Russell asked.

"More normal than you'd think. If the information's good, the CIs get paid for it. Whenever they're short of cash, they come up with something worth selling."

Leyton took another pastry, thank goodness. Otherwise I might have been tempted to take up comfort eating.

"Who found the body?" he asked.

"The police. Someone called triple zero before I got there. A woman. She said she was walking her dog outside and heard a gunshot."

"Did you go to the scene?"

"I would have. I was on my way, but there was an incident three blocks in the other direction, and I got sent there instead."

"Any connection?"

"I don't think so. The incident was DV-related. Domestic violence," I added for Russell's benefit. "A guy slapped his girlfriend for talking back to him, except she was making dinner at the time, and it got real messy."

"What did she do?" Leyton asked. "Go after him with a carving knife?"

"No, she emptied a pan of minestrone over his head, but she took it right off the stove, so it was hot, and..." My nose wrinkled as I recalled the way his skin had blistered. The way soup splashed across the floor like vomit. "I only eat gazpacho now."

"Guess I can understand that. So..." Leyton paused for a moment as he worked up to the big question. The sixty-four-thousand-dollar question, except that night had cost me everything. "So, why would the police think you killed a guy? How did Michael set you up?"

CHAPTER 3 - KYLIE

HOW DID MICHAEL set me up? With careful planning, calculation, and a mean streak far longer than his dick.

"He planted evidence at the scene. A long blonde hair on the body and another near the sink, plus my coffee cup in the trash. Then there was the circumstantial evidence—I'd told a couple of people I was going to meet a CI in that area."

"It's hardly damning, is it? If you'd been at the scene, you could easily have explained the forensics away as carelessness."

"Michael was the one who made sure I wasn't at the scene. *He* sent me to the soup incident. And the coffee cup? The last time I got coffee from that place, I was with Owen."

"Owen being...?" Russell asked.

"Senior Constable Owen Mills. He and Shane Chapman—Constable Chapman—were tight with Michael. And Owen must've kept my cup."

"Are you sure the cup and the hair were yours?"

"The cup had my name written on it."

"There're plenty of Kylies in Australia."

"It also had my shade of lipstick on the rim. And I knew. I just knew. Call it gut or intuition or whatever, but I just knew."

"A good lawyer could've got you off. Why run?"

"Because of the gun. Not only did Michael rig the scene, he hid the bloody murder weapon in my kitchen."

"Okay, that's a whole other level. How did you find it?"

"I couldn't sleep from worrying about the rest of the evidence, so I went to get a glass of water in the middle of the night. When I turned on the light, I saw one of the baseboards was loose, and I clipped it back into place. That's what you do, right? But then I started wondering *why* it was loose, so I pried it away, and that was when I found the pistol, wrapped in newspaper. Because everyone knows paper's the best way to preserve forensics."

"It was definitely the murder weapon?"

"I didn't know for certain at the time, but why else would it have been there? And yes, it was. I read about it online when I was in Honduras."

"Nobody else had access to your house?"

"Not between me going to bed and waking up, and the baseboard was fine when I made dinner. I notice stuff like that."

Or at least, I used to before stress turned my brain to mush.

Now Mimi chipped in for the first time in precise, clipped words. "At that point, why didn't you take the gun and dispose of it? With the main piece of evidence gone, you could have dealt with Michael later."

"Firstly, because if I got caught with the gun on my person, it would've been even more damning, and secondly, because whoever murdered Jasper John did a thorough job of it. According to the autopsy, the gunshot killed him, but he also had knife wounds. The knife's still missing, and coincidentally, so is one of the steak knives from the set my parents gave me for my twentieth birthday."

"Your parents gave you steak knives for your birthday?"

"Mum delegated to Dad, okay?" I wasn't sure I liked Mimi. She sounded all judgey.

"What kind of gun was it?"

"A Smith & Wesson .22 with a silencer attached."

"Not yours?"

"No, but the month before, the four of us were at the gun club—me, Michael, Shane, and Owen—and Shane brought that exact model of gun but without the silencer. I borrowed it, shot a handful of rounds, and put it back in the case myself. *My fingerprints were on it.*"

Shane had even wiped it down before he gave it to me, I remembered. Said he'd been eating crisps and wanted to get rid of the greasy finger marks. Stupid me had thought he was just being a gentleman. They must've been laughing at me behind my back for weeks.

"What was Michael's motive for framing you? If the relationship had gone sour, why not simply split up? One of you could have been reassigned."

"I didn't realise the relationship *had* gone sour. Looking back, I think he only started dating me so he could keep tabs." That and the fact he could fuck me whenever he wanted. "But we'd had a few differences of opinion at work. He'd let some tips slide rather than following them up and gone after other people with little to no evidence. That's why I think he was acting on somebody else's orders. And after Jasper John's murder, I heard rumours on the street that John knew of a dirty cop. Of course, everyone thinks that was me, that he'd cooked up a blackmail scheme that led me to kill him, but what if it was Michael? What if the night John asked to meet me, he wanted to turn Michael in?"

Mimi simply nodded. "You're right. You're fucked. I would've run too."

Gee, thanks for that, lady. Now I was certain I didn't like her.

Mimi glared at Leyton, and I wondered if he'd kicked her under the table. I'd have been tempted to do so myself if the table hadn't been so wide.

"I'll agree the evidence against you is fairly compelling," Leyton said, showing slightly more tact than his colleague. "Is there anything that supports your side of things? Anything at all? Emmy mentioned a phone in a lockbox?"

"I took Michael's phone when I left the house. I thought there might be something on it, messages maybe, but he used an app called Ether to talk to Owen and Shane, and at the time, I wasn't sure I'd be able to access anything useful."

Leyton sucked in a breath. "Ether? We can't do anything with that either. Believe me, we've tried."

So had every law enforcement agency in the world, all to no avail. Encrypted messages sent via Ether vanished five minutes after they were read, never to be seen again. Try to sidestep the app's security, and it fried your device. No wonder it had become a firm favourite with terrorists and criminals the world over.

"That's where Russell comes in. He can access the messages, but he needs the phone physically in his possession."

Now Leyton stared at Russell with newfound respect. "You can break into Ether? How the hell do you manage that?"

"Trade secret, I'm afraid."

A secret I was privy to. Ether was Russell's app. He'd created it for fun at school, hiding behind the name Kaito Nakamura, mostly because he enjoyed the challenge of coding but also as a way to chat to his mates without the teachers finding out. Now he was struggling to deal with the damage it had done. In Virginia, he'd wanted to pull the plug on the whole thing, but it seemed that someone had talked him out of it. I wasn't sure why.

"We've got another ongoing murder case right now, and we're sure the suspects communicated over Ether. Can you...?"

"Get me the phones, and I'll get you the messages."

Leyton glanced at Mimi, and she nodded once.

"Crikey, this is big. Access to Ether could solve so many crimes. Do the police know you can do this?"

"Not yet."

Not yet? He was planning to tell them? Offer his services? Leyton was right—this *was* big. Think of all the good that information could do in the right hands— I may have been less than enamoured with the QPS, but there were plenty of other police departments worldwide that weren't quite so rotten. Still, I couldn't afford to get distracted by the future—for the moment, I needed to focus on my case.

"So there's the phone, and I'm hoping it might be the smoking gun, so to speak. The only other thing in my favour is that the caller who reported the murder said she saw a man running from the scene. No doubt they'll try to twist it and say I was wearing trousers, but it still casts a little doubt."

"Did they ever trace the caller?"

"No, and we questioned everyone who owned a dog within a half-mile radius."

I was the one who'd pushed for that, before the evidence of my guilt began to pile up. Not one dog owner would admit to being in the area. Either they'd walked their pooches in a different direction or they were lying, and I wasn't sure which. I'd wanted to expand the search, but Superintendent Clarke had vetoed it, citing a lack of resources. I believe his exact words were, "We're not wasting any more time on a two-bit drug dealer." Although he'd soon changed his tune once he thought I'd killed the man and a common-or-garden murder threatened to turn into a scandal for the department.

But as far as I knew, the superintendent's subsequent efforts had centred around a PR campaign rather than further attempts to find the real culprit, no doubt steered by Michael and his band of merry men.

"So the key piece of evidence is the phone," Leyton said. "Where is it?"

Therein lay the problem. The phone was the reason I'd had to return to Australia in the first place, the reason I couldn't just have stayed in Virginia, hiding out in Emmy's mansion.

"I needed to put it somewhere safe. If I got arrested at the airport, I was worried it'd conveniently disappear."

"And?"

"It's in a safe deposit box. I stopped at the bank first thing on the morning I left, took out money to buy a new passport, and left the phone behind."

The passport guy was suspicious as hell when I'd turned up with cash—me, a serving police officer. It took twenty minutes to convince him it wasn't a sting. Then he'd laughed his head off and reinvented me as Tegan Wallace in return for eight thousand dollars and a promise not to arrest him if I ever came back. He didn't like Michael either, which was probably why he'd kept my secret all these years.

"You already had a safe deposit box?" Leyton asked.

"I got it a few years previously to store my grandma's jewellery." The salesman at the bank had talked me into signing up for a long-term discounted plan, paid by direct debit each month. "I used to keep it at home, but then I disturbed a burglar in my old apartment, and I didn't want to take the chance anymore. It was the one thing I couldn't replace."

"You brought the key?"

"Sort of. It has fingerprint access." State of the art, according to the brochure. Now, I wished I'd stuck with old-fashioned. "I have to go myself, with ID. And I'd bet my grandma's gold necklace that Michael's been to the bank and asked them to call the cops if I ever show up."

Russell had already lost most of his tan from Egypt, and now he turned a shade paler. "Is it really wise to continue with this? Perhaps it'd be better for you to go back to America and lie low?"

I'd had the same thought a hundred times myself, but I was sick of running. Sick of pretending to be someone I wasn't, and today, for the first time, I had help with my problem.

"I can't. I have to try and clear my name."

Even if it killed me. Living a lie was no life at all.

Leyton looked at Mimi, and she shrugged. A woman of few words, it seemed, and those she spoke were generally unpleasant.

"We'll make a plan," he said. "Give us a day or two."

CHAPTER 4 - KYLIE

TODAY WAS THE day. Monday, the start of a brand new week, and I'd spent the weekend alternately plotting with Leyton and pacing the villa while Russell continued his love affair with his laptop.

Except this morning, Russell looked different.

"What's with the glasses?" I asked him.

"Eyestrain. The optician says I should wear them more often, but I find if I do, my eyes get lazy."

He'd gone for thick plastic frames, hipster chic, and they were weirdly...hot. But in a daggy sort of way, obviously, because this was work and I wasn't meant to be thinking about stuff like that.

"Ah," was the best I could come up with.

"Coffee?"

"You're a mind reader."

How long until Leyton arrived? Ten minutes, according to the ridiculously ornate clock on the living room wall. According to Akeem, the thing had been designed by an "up-and-coming Indonesian guy, so talented, he'll be famous one day, and then Emmy'll have to admit the clock was an excellent purchase, even though she hates it."

At first, I couldn't understand how Akeem had overridden Emmy, but then he'd somehow convinced me that going to the spa yesterday was a "fabulous" idea. The poor masseuse got all apologetic when she found so many knots in my muscles that she didn't know where to start, but at least my skin would look clear for my mug shot.

I sipped my coffee on the terrace, trying to enjoy what could be my last morning of freedom. The plan called for me to go into the bank alone, and if the staff tried to stall me, I'd push them to hurry, say I'd leave otherwise. They'd call the police, of course they would, and letting me access my box quickly was a better prospect than losing me completely.

Leyton had paid a visit on Friday, posing as a customer, and we knew there was a fire exit at the back of the building. Blackwood would have a second car there as a backup while Leyton waited for me out front. Meanwhile, they'd monitor the police radio traffic with scanners to get an idea of when I had to run.

Was I scared? No, I was terrified, but I still had to do this.

Leyton arrived right on time and declined an offer of coffee. Was his adrenaline flowing already? My heart had begun battering my ribcage the moment I woke up. Before I left, Russell gave me an awkward hug, a sort of cross between "good luck" and "goodbye."

"See you later, Ky."

Later back at the resort or later in court? Oh, who was I kidding? Russell wouldn't stick around for court. With his part of the job over, he'd be on the first plane back to England.

"Yeah. Later."

The butterflies were back with a vengeance, and I headed for the door, wanting to get the trip over with. But Leyton didn't move.

"Have you got the key for the Mustang?" he asked.

"We're taking the Mustang? Won't that stand out?"

"Sometimes, it's better to hide in plain sight. If people remember seeing us, they'll pay attention to the car, not its occupants. Plus it's faster."

His unspoken words: if we need to make a run for it.

But he spoke the truth about people's memories. How many times had I questioned a witness, only for them to remember some insignificant detail of no use to anyone? After one bank robbery, I spoke to six people who all described the suspect's orange baseball cap perfectly, but couldn't tell me anything about the man wearing it, not even his skin colour. We found the cap on the pavement right outside the bank. Never did find the suspect.

Would the Mustang have the same effect? If nothing else, it was the automobile equivalent of a death row inmate's final meal. Might as well go out in style, right?

And at least Mimi wasn't with us. She'd graced us with her presence yesterday while Leyton and I went over the last details of the plan, only to insist I switched my messenger bag for a backpack and change some of the timings. Now I'd get the final call to leave one minute before the critical point rather than the two minutes Leyton had pushed for.

"Can I drive there?" I asked as we walked along the winding path towards the carport. Leyton's legs were longer than mine, and I had to hurry to keep up. He didn't seem particularly keen on the idea, but after a moment of hesitation, he nodded.

"Just make sure you stick to the speed limits. We

don't want to get pulled over before we even reach the city."

"Cross my heart."

We reached the Mustang, and I inhaled the rich scent of leather as I slid behind the wheel. Emmy had picked every available option, from upgraded speakers to tinted windows to horse logos embossed on the headrests. Even on my old salary, it would have taken me years to save for a car like that. Right now, I'd struggle to buy a bicycle.

Leyton's phone buzzed, and he checked the screen.

"Just Mimi. Everything's quiet around the bank."

"Who is Mimi, exactly?" I asked him as I did up my seat belt. The V8 engine started with a throaty roar.

"Why do you ask?"

"Because *she* doesn't strike me as the kind of girl who sticks to the limits."

When we first met, I'd assumed she was Leyton's assistant, but I'd changed my mind on that. I couldn't see her taking orders from anybody.

Leyton just chuckled. "As far as Mimi's concerned, there are no limits. Now, let's go over this plan one more time."

My guts threatened to heave their contents all over the pavement as I stood outside the bank. Was this how career criminals felt each time they broke the law? Scared as hell and sweating through their clothes? What about Michael? Did the guilt eat away at him? Or did it slide off smoothly like raindrops on a windscreen?

Deep breaths, Kylie. I had to go inside because nothing looked more suspicious than hanging around on the street, and Leyton was by the kerb thirty metres along the road, waiting for me to make my move. One man had already stopped to admire the Mustang.

In the air-conditioned silence, I lined up, then asked to speak to the manager about accessing a safe deposit box.

"Your name, ma'am?"

"I'd rather speak to the manager."

"If I could just give him your name…"

"I'll give *him* my name. And I'm in a hurry, so if you'd just get him, I'd be grateful."

The agent flounced away, no doubt muttering a few choice words under her breath. I couldn't allow myself the luxury of caring. Instead, I forced myself to uncurl my fists and settle onto a seat, giving the illusion of nonchalance. What if they had a photo of me? Would they check every customer?

Every second felt like a decade until a man in an ill-fitting grey suit strode towards me. Once he got close enough for me to read his badge, the iron band around my chest loosened a millimetre. *Barney Kemp, Branch Manager.* Yes, that was the man whose picture Russell had shown me earlier.

"Ma'am? I understand you want to access a safe deposit box?"

"That's right."

"Is it your box?"

"It is."

"Well, I can certainly help you with that. Do you have the box number and your ID?"

This was the moment of truth… Did he know? "It's

box number 864," I said, holding my passport out. My real passport. I'd kept it with me all this time, hidden in the lining of my suitcase. "And as I said to your assistant, I'm in a hurry."

Oh, he knew. He snatched my passport and took a step back as he checked the pages, stammering, "I-I-If you'll excuse me, I'll just run our security checks."

"Last time, the manager checked my documents at the terminal right here and took me down to the vault."

"Uh, yes. Yes, I'm sure he did. But we recently changed our procedures, and...and, uh, I have to do some secondary checks."

I plucked my passport out of his grasp. "I'm sure you'll understand if I don't want to let this out of my sight. One can never be too careful nowadays."

"I do understand. I-I-I'll be right back."

"Sure. And I meant what I said about being in a hurry. If you're not back in two minutes, I'll have to leave."

"Two minutes. Yes, got it."

He tripped as he hurried away and barely caught himself on the edge of a table. A white-haired lady waiting in line for the ATM gave me a curious look, and I managed what I hoped was a snooty smile.

"Just can't get the service these days."

"Patience is a virtue, young lady."

And nosiness was a pain in the ass. I turned away in a huff as Leyton spoke into my earpiece.

"You're doing good, Ky. Thirty seconds down."

Barney Kemp didn't return in two minutes. He took closer to four, and at three minutes, Leyton sounded the alarm.

"Units despatched to the bank."

Oh, hell. I wanted to run, but I couldn't. I had to stand my ground. Keep a neutral expression and pretend nothing was wrong as Kemp led the way to the vault, step by painfully slow step. I wanted to yell at him to hurry up, but I bit my tongue while he fumbled with his key, almost dropping the damn thing before he turned it with a hand trembling worse than mine.

"Thank you."

"I'll be right outside, ma'am."

"Ky, you have to leave now," Leyton said in my ear. "The cops are ninety seconds away."

Bless him, he'd given me thirty seconds more than Mimi had decreed, but I couldn't leave. Not now. Not when I was so bloody close.

I pressed my finger to the sensor, yanked the drawer open, then shrugged out of my backpack. There it was—Michael's phone, right where I'd left it, plus five little boxes with my grandma's jewellery and a bronze sculpture of my childhood dog that my grandpa had made. I'd loved that damn dog. I shoved the whole lot in the bag because whatever happened, I'd never be coming back.

"Ky, get out! They're close. Too close."

I ran. Out of the vault, past a terrified Barney Kemp, up the stairs, and into the bank. Every head turned to stare at me, but nobody moved as I sprinted for the door.

"Thirty seconds. Oh, shit."

Shit indeed. There was the Mustang, exactly where I'd left it, but between me and the car, Shane Chapman jogged along the pavement, and the moment his gaze locked onto me, it felt as if all the air had been sucked out of my body.

The Mustang rolled forward, but Leyton couldn't get to me. The car was pointing the wrong way, and by the time he turned it around, I'd be cuffed on the ground. Why hadn't I gone out of the damn fire escape? There was another Blackwood car waiting behind the building, and if I just managed to reach it...

I spun and ran.

Shane's footsteps pounded after me as I ducked down the alley at the side of the building, dodging a pile of trash that spilled across the concrete. Could I make it? Shane used to run track in high school, but he'd eaten too many donuts in the years since. Lost shape.

A glimmer of hope shone as the far end of the alley grew closer, only to darken like a shadow across the sun as Owen Mills appeared in front of me. Oh, hell. Oh hell, oh hell, oh hell! I stood a chance taking one of them on, but not both. Where was Leyton? Would he come to help?

Then Owen dived to the side as a motorbike nearly ran him down. A dirt bike, the rider's face obscured by a black visor as it skidded to a halt in front of me. What the hell?

"Well? What the fuck are you waiting for?"

Hold on. I recognised that voice.

"Mimi?"

"Well, it's not the bloody tooth fairy."

I swung a leg over the back, then grabbed Mimi's waist as she twisted the throttle and floored it towards Shane. Would she go left or right? Neither, it turned out. She aimed straight for him, speeding up, leaving him no choice but to leap sideways into a pile of junk.

Then we were zooming along the main road. Sirens

sounded as police cars turned to follow, and what did
Mimi do? She laughed. The crazy bitch actually
laughed.

Me? I shrieked as she rode down the centre line,
missing an oncoming truck by inches.

"Don't worry," Leyton told me through my earpiece.
"Mimi's been in police chases before."

So had I, but always from the other side. "They'll
get more cars. The helicopter..."

"The helicopter's grounded for repairs. Your bigger
problem is that Shane Chapman's just commandeered
a souped-up sports bike, and he's coming after you."

Mimi leaned into one turn after the other, and I
muttered a prayer under my breath. I didn't even have
a helmet. And neither did Shane when I took a look
behind us. He was catching us fast, and his expression
was a mixture of determination and anger. Mimi
skidded through another street, and the police cars
dropped back, but when I risked another glance, Shane
was only a hundred metres away. A hundred metres
with a red light dead ahead.

Oh, hell. Would Mimi stop? Cars whizzed across the
intersection, oblivious. She had to stop, right? Then the
light went green, and Mimi accelerated once more.
We'd ended up on a road with a dozen traffic lights, a
road where I knew most of the side streets led to dead-
ends, and every single light turned green as we
approached. Was this some sort of divine intervention?
Maybe, but Shane was taking advantage of it. Mimi's
bike might have had the edge on agility, but Shane's
was faster, and he was gaining. One more light, one
more light...

We sped through, and I heard the roar of Shane's

engine closing. Then the screech of brakes, the crunch of metal, and a sickening thud. Fuck! Mimi eased off on the throttle, and I twisted to see. Had someone run a red light? Because Shane's bike was embedded in the side of a truck, and the bloodstain splashed across the logo for *Brisbane's Best Vegetables* didn't look good.

"Shame," Mimi said. "He should've worn a helmet."

"I'm not wearing a freaking helmet either!"

"Yes, but I'm driving, and I don't crash."

She set off, accelerating more slowly this time. The road was blocked now thanks to Shane, so the other cops following would be delayed as they tried to find a way around. I began to breathe again.

"Holy shit," I mumbled. "What just happened?"

"That there was karma in action."

"Do you think Shane's dead?"

"I expect so. He was doing a hundred and thirty kilometres per hour, so unless his skull's made of titanium..." She signalled and took a left into a residential street, so quiet in the daytime while people were at work. One man glanced up from watering his garden, and I quickly turned my head.

"Gonna need a pickup," Mimi said, presumably speaking to Blackwood. "Send whoever's close."

Pickup? I needed a defibrillator.

She stopped the bike beside a small park and kicked down the stand, then hopped off in a smooth move a gymnast would've been proud of.

"You can get down now."

She made it sound so easy. My knees buckled as my feet touched the ground, and I clutched at the bike for support. *Don't stumble, Kylie.* Falling in front of Mimi would be the cherry on top of this disaster of a day. I used to think I was tough, but three years had worn me down, and the events in Egypt had taken their toll too. Now I was tired. I longed to sleep and never wake up.

"What about your bike? Are you leaving it here?"

"I stole it this morning, so probably someone should give it back to the owner."

She strode off into the park, leaving me scrambling to catch up.

"You *stole* it?"

"What, you think I'd use my own vehicle in a police chase? That's such an amateur move."

"What if you'd damaged it?"

"I didn't." Mimi hopped onto a swing and began swinging back and forth, not a care in the world. "The owner should thank me—that thing's notorious now. I bet we made every news station, and that's got to add a couple of hundred bucks to the value."

"You're insane."

"Sanity is in the eye of the beholder."

"We were in a police chase. A cop most likely died. Until today, I hadn't actually committed a crime, and now they're gonna try even harder to catch me."

"Just a temporary glitch." She waved a hand, dismissive, as I clutched the swing set's wooden frame to stop my knees from buckling. "You gotta look at the long term. When we nail Michael and his buddies, one less trial will be needed. A casket's cheaper than a bunch of lawyers. And the savings could fund a whole lot of new playground equipment like this stuff. Kids need something to keep them occupied."

Well, this beholder thought Mimi Tran was out of her bloody mind. But if she cared, she didn't show it, just swung higher and higher until suddenly, she leapt clear in midair and landed like a cat.

"Our ride's here."

I turned to see a green minivan parked at the edge of the road. Could I even walk that far? I'd have to crawl if not, because Mimi wasn't waiting.

CHAPTER 5 - KYLIE

THE MUSTANG WAS already back in its parking spot when the minivan pulled up outside the hotel. Apart from nodding a hello, the driver had ignored me the whole trip, and Mimi had mostly spoken into her phone, in code, it seemed. Either that or she was arranging a date. Drama, dinner, and spirits were all mentioned, and I wasn't sure whether the last was in reference to hard liquor or the dearly departed. I also wasn't sure I wanted to find out.

"Uh, I need to thank you—" I started, but she cut me off.

"Forget it. For me, it was just work."

"But—"

"I need to get back to the office. Don't forget your bag."

That was it: dismissed. I staggered out of the vehicle, heading for the path to the villa, only for Leyton to make me jump out of my skin when he appeared between the trees.

"What the...?"

"Here, let me take this." He wrapped an arm around my waist and liberated my backpack with his other hand. "You don't look too steady."

"You scared me half to death!"

"Sorry about that."

"And you left me with a crazy woman," I whisper-shouted, keeping an eye out for stray tourists. "Why didn't you warn me her elevator doesn't go all the way to the top?"

"I apologise for that too."

"I nearly died from a heart attack."

"Mimi may have a screw loose, but she gets the job done."

"Screw loose? She stole a motorbike and outran half of the QPS. What happened to Shane? Is he dead?"

"Nobody's confirmed it, but I believe so."

We reached the villa, and I didn't bother to fight with the door, just followed the path around the side and collapsed onto one of the sun loungers on the terrace. A man I'd worked with, hung out with, and shared my life with was dead. I should have felt awful, but after the way he'd treated me at the end, I couldn't bring myself to care. Did that make me a terrible person?

"Hey." Russell settled on the edge of the sun lounger and brushed the hair away from my face. "I heard what happened. It's all over the TV."

This got worse and worse. "My face?"

"Not while you were on the bike—it was too blurry —but they've got an old picture of you with blonde hair."

"Shit."

"You look very different now." He ran his fingers through my hair again. "The fringe changes your whole face, and you're thinner too."

"Shane's dead."

"Yes. Someone put a clip of his body on YouTube."

Yeuch. Did nobody have compassion anymore? I

may not have liked Shane, but he had a mother and a sister, and neither of them deserved to see him like that.

"They should take that down."

"I've already reported it. Ky, what can I do to help? You're not going into shock, are you?" He pulled his phone out of his pocket. "I should check the symptoms for that."

"I'm just a bit dazed. What happened is still sinking in, I think."

"Shall I get you a drink? A blanket?"

I felt too sick to swallow, and it was twenty-five degrees in the shade. What I really wanted was to curl up in my childhood bedroom, for my mum to wrap me up in her arms and tell me everything was going to be okay. But that was impossible, and a sob escaped just from thinking about it.

"Ky?"

"Could I...? Could I have a hug?"

That way, I could pretend somebody cared, just for a few minutes, even if that hug was slightly stiff and planned rather than spontaneous. I closed my eyes as Russell enveloped me, trying to imagine my mum's floral perfume instead of Russell's musky scent. It felt weird at first, but he didn't let go, holding me tighter as I relaxed, and I had to concede that geek or not, Russell gave really good hugs.

Then I caught movement from the corner of my eye, and Leyton appeared in the doorway.

"I've plugged the phone in to charge. When you're ready, we should have a debrief, but take your time. It's been a tough day."

"A debrief? Can't you just watch the chase on TV

instead? People were filming it, apparently."

"I've already seen the chase. Mimi was streaming it in real-time. It's what happens now that we need to talk about. The cops know you're back in Australia, and after today's chaos in the city, they're gonna redouble their efforts to catch you."

"We made it worse, didn't we? I should've stayed away."

"Sometimes, things have to get worse before they can get better."

"How can this possibly get better? Not only am I wanted for killing Jasper John, now they'll try to pin Shane's death on me too."

Because I wouldn't tell them who Mimi was, even if they threatened me. She'd only been trying to help in her own, warped way, and if she hadn't picked me up, I'd have been languishing in jail at that moment instead of fidgeting on the terrace at the Black Diamond Resort.

"Shane's death was an accident. The police have rules for car chases—you know that better than I do— and he broke all of them because he was following his own agenda."

"I'm not sure the judge'll see it that way."

"It won't get to court."

"Maybe if I run again…"

"Don't run." Leyton held out a hand. "Come inside and let's see what we might have to trade."

Russell followed, making a beeline for Michael's phone. The old Samsung looked clunky beside Russell's newer model, a relic from the past. What was on there? Was Leyton right? Could we really find something to trade? Deals got done all the time by people way above my pay grade—two-bit criminals bartering their freedom in exchange for enough information to catch a bigger fish. What could I offer?

Fortunately, I knew Michael's PIN. I'd seen him type it in enough times, and I guess he thought I was too dumb to remember.

"The code's 5326."

"Thanks."

Although having seen Russell in action, I had a feeling that even if I didn't have the PIN, the security wouldn't do much more than slow him down.

I'd seen him do his Ether trick once before, in Egypt, and to my non-techie eyes, it seemed as if he used the same method in Queensland. First, he opened the system settings in Michael's Ether app and typed in a ridiculously long code from memory. Then a box flashed up with another code—a mix of letters and numbers, twenty or so.

His fingers flew over the keys of his laptop, opening up a database full of nonsense, what looked like a cross between Russian and Wingdings. Only when he entered the password from the phone did parts of it decode into English.

"I only get two minutes to enter the decryption key," he explained. "Otherwise it resets."

"What happens if you can't type fast enough?"

"I can."

Yes, he could.

There were six thousand lines in Michael's record. He'd sent a lot of messages over the years, but would it be enough? I held my breath as Russell scrolled back to the fifteenth of February, just over three years ago. I'd never forget that date. It was the day two lives had ended, mine and Jasper John's.

The downside of Russell's Ether methodology was that we could only see Michael's messages, not those he was replying to. But the usernames were there—three of them, and one of them was mine. Back then, I'd used Ether too. After working a case where a girl had been held to ransom over naked selfies she'd sent an ex, I'd figured the app would give me peace of mind over my own dirty messages.

Funny how time could dull your memories, wasn't it?

In the years I'd been abroad, I'd avoided thinking about my own Ether messages with Michael, and with practice, I'd managed to block out our entire train wreck of a relationship. But now, as I perched on the edge of a chair next to Russell, those final weeks came crashing back.

"Who's JayebirdAU?" he asked. "Is that you?"

"Uh, yes. My middle name's Jaye." Which he probably already knew

And right then, I wished I'd gone to Bahrain instead of Australia. Or China, or Iraq, or even back to Russia. Anywhere but an upmarket resort in Australia where a computer geek and a private investigator were staring at the screen with widening eyes.

Of course, they could only read Michael's side of the conversation, but my username was in the "participants" field, and it didn't take a genius to fill in the blanks.

Bossman: Nice choice of words, babe. Tell me how you want me to fuck you.

JayebirdAU: *******************************

Bossman: With that view of your perfect ass...

JayebirdAU: ********************************

Bossman: Oh, so you like that? I'll get my hand warmed up.

JayebirdAU: ********************************

Bossman: Why would I want to stop you from screaming my name?

JayebirdAU: ********************************

Bossman: Who cares about the neighbours? I want everyone to know you're mine.

JayebirdAU: ********************************

Bossman: In that case, I'll come inside your filthy little mouth, and you're gonna swallow every drop.

JayebirdAU: ********************************

Bossman: Not until late tonight, babe. Touch yourself while you think of me.

I wanted to sink into the floor. Actually, that was too tame. Death would've been preferable. *Come back, Egypt, all is forgiven.* I couldn't look at either of the men. Not only were the details of my sex life splashed across the screen, so was the evidence of my poor judgement, and that was actually worse.

Russell cleared his throat and hastily scrolled down to the next block of messages. They started just after 8 p.m., a group chat between Michael, Duke916, and SurfsUp, the latter two parties otherwise known as Shane Chapman and Owen Mills respectively.

I forced myself to forget the memories of Michael's slimy touch and read.

Duke916: ********************************

Bossman: Alone?

Duke916: *******************************
Bossman: How's the street looking?
Shane: *******************************
Bossman: Fucking mutts.
Duke916: *******************************
SurfsUp: *******************************
Bossman: Can't. If he talks to Ky, we're fucked. I'll go in the back way.
SurfsUp: *******************************
Bossman: Who cares? I'm gonna knock anyway.
Duke916: *******************************

Michael had gone quiet for half an hour, according to the timestamps. Long enough to kill a man, plant enough evidence to incriminate me, and clean up? If he hurried, yes.

Bossman: It's done.
Duke916: *******************************
Bossman: Yeah. Gonna pick up a pizza on my way home.
SurfsUp: *******************************
Bossman: Nah, Ky gets grouchy if I'm late.
SurfsUp: *******************************
Duke916: *******************************
SurfsUp: *******************************
Bossman: Only if you want it to come with STDs. Get tested lately, asshole?
SurfsUp: *******************************
Bossman: Call Froggy, would ya? Tell him we're on for tomorrow.
SurfsUp: *******************************
Bossman: Make it 19.30. Clarke wants me to talk

to some Sheila from the news at the end of the shift.
    Duke916: *******************************
    Bossman: Depends if her knockers are as good as the last one.

A tear leaked down my cheek as I got to the end. That was it. The chat finished for the night. For three years, I'd thought that if I could get into Michael's messages, if I could just find out what he'd been talking about with Shane and Owen that evening, I'd be able to prove my innocence and his guilt. But this...it wasn't enough. Reading between the lines, I knew what had happened—Michael had killed Jasper John then calmly stopped for takeout on his way home. But I couldn't prove it. And what was that bit about the knockers at the end? Had he slept with a reporter?

A bullet wasn't kind enough for that asshole. Even now, he could still stick a knife in. Those words, those few short sentences? They wouldn't convince a jury.

CHAPTER 6 - KYLIE

NOT ENOUGH, NOT enough, not enough...

I grabbed the mouse and scanned the messages for the week before the murder. And the week after. There was plenty about cricket, beer, a couple of ongoing cases, and a surfing trip Michael, Shane, and Owen planned to take, the chatter interspersed with comments about women that showed a misogynistic side they'd kept hidden from me. But no mention of Jasper John's death.

Despair coursed through my veins. For three years, I'd been hoping, and it *wasn't enough*.

"The only vaguely incriminating part is where he mentions being fucked if someone talks to me," I said. "But any half-decent lawyer could cast doubt on that, couldn't they?"

Leyton blew out a breath before he spoke. "I hate to say it, but I agree with you. Michael could tell a jury he was planning to throw you a surprise party. Buy you a gift. Take you on a trip."

"What about the time?" Russell asked. "The ME put Jasper John's death between seven thirty and eight thirty."

How did he know that? "You read the autopsy report?"

"I got curious."

"A coincidence," Leyton said. "Yes, the time and the part about someone talking to Kylie fit, and even the mention of dogs on the street outside, but it's all tenuous. Who's Froggy?"

I'd never heard that name. "Sorry. I have no idea."

"I'll speak to our lawyers. Get a second opinion."

Leyton's words spoke of hope, but his tone didn't.

"Don't worry, we both know what they'll say. I knew it was a gamble coming back here." I snatched up my backpack to give my hands something to do—it was either that or tear my hair out. "Thank you for trying, both of you. I guess deep down I always figured this would catch up with me, and I...I..."

A sob welled up in my throat, and I hurried into my bedroom before I broke apart completely. What should I do now? Face the music or run? I still had Tegan's passport as well as Kyanna's, but the airports would be on high alert, and my photo was splashed across every news channel. If a cop didn't spot me, a member of the public would.

I emptied the contents of the bag onto the bed, and the tears flowed freely as I took Grandma's favourite necklace out of its velvet box. The diamonds twinkled around the emerald in the middle as I held it up to the light. The setting was a bit scratched now, but the stones still shone as brightly as the first time I'd seen it around her neck. The piece had been a gift from Grandpa on their tenth wedding anniversary. Emerald green to match her eyes, a colour I'd inherited. She'd worn that necklace every day until she gave it to me on the afternoon I graduated from the police academy. I remembered her words perfectly—*you've got the know-how to keep this safe now, young lady*. Her engagement and wedding rings, her sapphire brooch, and a ruby necklace came to me when she died. Where would I keep them when I went to prison? I should've left them in the safe deposit box.

The bronze dog stared up at me. Shadow, he'd been called, because he always followed me around the house. Going to the bathroom was slightly awkward, but mostly his devotion was sweet. Before my grandpa's eyesight went, he'd made a living as an artist, a sculptor, although he'd usually worked on a much larger scale. Several of his works graced the streets and gardens of Brisbane, and back when I'd had freedom, I liked to take a tour of them each year on the anniversary of his passing. Now I just had Shadow. I put him on the chest of drawers opposite the bed. Perhaps Emmy would take care of him for me?

Eyes still prickling, I sat on the covers, knees drawn up to my chin. What now? I couldn't stay at the resort forever, and even if I could, the villa would be nothing but a fancy jail cell. But what if I lay low for a month, maybe two, then left the country again? Yes, I know I said I wanted to stop running, but before the debacle at the bank and my near-death experience with Mimi, I'd had a modicum of hope. All that had changed with the police hot on my tail... How long would the authorities watch for me? Dammit, they had facial recognition cameras everywhere at the airports, and they wouldn't be fooled by contacts or a new hairstyle if I flew commercial. Would Emmy let me borrow the jet again? Even now, my debt to that woman was so high I'd never pay it off.

A soft knock interrupted my pity fest, and I swallowed down a sniffle before I answered.

"What?"

"Can I come in?" Russell asked.

"If you must." Shit, now I sounded like a bitch, and he'd done nothing but help me. "Sorry. Yes, come in."

The door opened slowly, as if he didn't really want to be there, and I couldn't blame him. I didn't want to be there either.

"Sorry you didn't find the answers you were looking for."

"Thanks for trying."

He perched awkwardly on the edge of the bed, and I grabbed the jewellery as it slid towards him.

"It was the least I could do." He picked up Grandma's engagement ring. "You got this from the bank?"

I nodded. "It belonged to my grandmother. The value's more sentimental than anything else, but..."

Dammit, another tear escaped.

"Shall I ask Akeem to put it in the hotel's safe?"

Should he? It was a nice offer, but how quickly would I be able to get it out again?

"I think I'd be better off keeping it with me."

Russell looked up sharply. "You're planning to run again?"

"Yes. No. I don't know. What other choice do I have?"

"Give Leyton a chance. He's only had the case for a few days."

"Michael's too careful to leave evidence."

"Everyone has chinks in their armour. Leyton's got Michael's messages as a starting point, plus a team of investigators and that crazy woman on the motorbike."

I held up one trembling hand, and a bubble of

hysterical laughter leaked out. "I'm still shaking from that."

Russell held up his own hand, and it had a definite quake too. "Join the club."

"Over and over, I just keep wondering what would have happened if that last set of lights had changed a few seconds earlier. Would I be the one lying in the morgue instead of Shane? I wasn't even wearing a helmet."

Although sometimes, the idea of a silk-lined casket didn't seem all that bad. At least my worries would be gone.

"Stop dwelling on it. The lights wouldn't have changed."

"You can't say that. Luck, that's all it was. Pure, dumb luck. If Mimi had ridden a tiny bit slower..."

Russell hesitated, then gave a sort of grimace followed by an apologetic little shrug. "No, it wasn't luck."

Huh? What was he talking about? He glanced out of the door, towards his laptop on the table, and the implications of what he'd said slowly sank in.

"You? *You* were controlling the traffic lights? How?"

"As I said, it's been a busy month. Brisbane City Council could do with improving its cybersecurity as well."

"What did you do? Turn the last light green for me and red for Shane?"

He nodded.

Bloody freaking hell. That split-second timing—he said the lights wouldn't have changed, but if he'd pushed the button just a second earlier... Wait. How *did* he know the right moment to switch the lights?

"I don't understand. Were you watching us? Was there a camera somewhere?"

"Not exactly."

"Then how...?"

"Everyone has their weakness, Kylie. Yours appears to be puppy pictures."

"What?" At first, I didn't understand. Then suddenly I did. Those cute pictures in my email. The cuter ones on the website I clicked through to because I needed cheering up. "You hacked my damn phone?"

He ducked to the side. "Please don't kill me."

Oh, it was tempting. So tempting. But one death that day was quite enough. Instead, I spoke through gritted teeth.

"Did you hijack my GPS?"

"Uh, yes. And your camera, microphone, and data signal too. Then I overlaid your location on the Traffic Management Centre's real-time map and made a few adjustments to their system. Sorry."

"I...I..." I didn't know what to say. Russell had killed a man. Not with his bare hands, but he'd still been responsible for Shane's death. "You did that for me?"

"When it came down to a choice between you and him, it really wasn't a hard decision." He gave a half-smile, just a flicker. "I've no doubt it was the right choice, but does the guilt get easier to live with?"

Until last month in Egypt, I'd only killed one person, a drugged-out lunatic waving a pistol who'd already fired three shots at me and my colleagues, all of whom thankfully lived. The shooting had given me a few restless nights, but to paraphrase Russell, it hadn't been a hard decision. Him or me. Then I found out he'd been beating his girlfriend for the last two years, and any guilt I might have felt vanished into the ether.

My time in Luxor, or rather, a small village nearby, had added five bodies to my tally. Sleep hadn't come so easily after that, as the dark circles under my eyes showed. Again, it had been a matter of survival, but those men still had families. Children.

No, the guilt remained strong over that disaster of a day.

Russell passed me a crisp white handkerchief—monogrammed with his initials—to wipe away the tears streaming down my cheeks. Oh, hell, I was a mess. I'd held it together in Virginia, back when I'd still had hope, but now everything just leaked out of me. Despair at the situation I was in. A hint of annoyance at Russell for invading my privacy. Fear for the future. Remorse for dragging so many others into my mess. Residual terror from the wild ride with Mimi. Sorrow that Russell had been forced to take a life to save me. But mostly anger at Michael for putting me into that position in the first place.

I wished it had been him on the sports bike.

"I want to tell you it gets easier, but right now..."

A shrug was the best I could manage. I barely even trusted myself to speak.

This time, Russell's hug didn't start out awkward like before, and I sagged against his chest, my energy spent.

"What if they realise it was you?" I mumbled into his shoulder.

"If they work out it was something other than a glitch, which is unlikely since I doctored the logs too, they'll trace the intrusion back to an internet café in

Saint Petersburg. Don't worry about me, Kylie."

Just hearing my real name hurt, and I struggled to regain my composure. Lost the battle. Why fight anymore? Instead, I gave in and lay down on the bed, broken, and let Russell hold me until I passed out from exhaustion.

CHAPTER 7 - KYLIE

I WOKE UP alone.

At first, I thought I'd dreamed Russell's presence, but when I rolled over, the faintest hint of his aftershave still lingered on the pillow. Something light —hints of cedar, saffron, grapefruit... Can you tell I worked summers behind the men's grooming counter at a department store before I became a cop?

That seemed like a lifetime ago now.

And unfortunately, the presence of eau de Russell meant breakfast promised to be an awkward affair. Should I apologise? Keep quiet and pretend my meltdown never happened? I put the decision off for half an hour while I soaked in the tub, savouring the near-scalding water and a mountain of bubbles. If I got caught, I'd probably never see a bath again. I might not even live long enough to take a shower, not when I'd helped to put a reasonable number of my fellow inmates behind bars.

I considered slipping under the water, inhaling, and ending it all right there. But then Michael would get away with what he'd done. And the only thing worse than facing life in prison was the prospect of my sleaze of an ex staying free.

The thought made me clench my fists so hard I ended up with a row of little red fingernail-dents marching across my palm. What kind of fucked-up world let a man escape a murder charge while an innocent woman had her life ruined?

When I slunk into the living room, I found a mug of lukewarm coffee waiting for me opposite Russell's three laptops. Yes, three. What were they doing, breeding overnight? Soft music played in the background, but where was Russell? A shadow passed behind the gauzy curtains blowing in the breeze from the terrace, back and forth, back and forth, back and forth. Curiosity got the better of me, and I got up to see why he was pacing, then realised he had a phone clamped to his ear. Was there another problem with the case?

"No, Mother, I'm not firing Finn's lawyer. If he wants different representation, he can do the deed himself."

A pause.

"Well, *you'll* have to pay for a new counsel, won't you? Just because he's my brother doesn't mean he deserves to escape punishment for his crimes. His actions almost got two women I care about killed, for crying out loud."

Two women he cared about? Tai was one of them, obviously—she and Russell had been sort-of dating before the incident at al-Nahas. Before she stopped arguing with Ren and hooked up with him instead. I was happy for them, honestly, but seeing them together in Virginia had only served to deepen the pain caused by my own failed relationship with Michael. Ren was so fiercely protective of her. So sweet with the way he put her first.

But who was the second woman Russell cared

about? Me? Only one other woman had survived, the Egyptian wife of the encampment's cook who'd hidden behind a water tank when the shooting started, and she didn't speak any English. So... Russell cared about me? That was...that was... Tears prickled because it had been so long since I'd had a true friend that I'd almost forgotten what it was like to be valued.

Outside, Russell's tone grew more exasperated. "Look, I didn't ask him to break the law. And how the hell was I supposed to know what he was doing?" A pause. "Yes, you do that."

He hung up abruptly, and I didn't have time to duck inside before he spun and caught me eavesdropping. Busted.

"Uhhhh..."

"Sorry about that."

Why was *he* apologising? "Was that your mother?"

He gave me a wry smile, accompanied by a roll of his eyes. "Nobody else can send my stress levels this high."

"What did she want?" Actually, that was none of my business. "Forget it, you don't have to answer."

"Apparently, the fact that my brother's in jail is my fault because I didn't stop him from—and I quote—being taken advantage of. Never mind that he hid all the bloody evidence."

"Well, that's the stupidest thing I've ever heard."

"Welcome to my life. The biggest mistake I ever made was thinking that Finn could change into anything but the spoilt brat I grew up with. But enough about him—how did you sleep?"

"I'm so sorry I got upset."

"After yesterday's drama, I think you were entitled

to."

"Still..." Oh, thank goodness. A knock at the door saved us from more awkwardness. "I'll get that."

I hoped for a housekeeper or even Akeem, but it was Leyton, complete with his own laptop bag and a bouquet of flowers. He held them out, quick to explain that they weren't actually from him.

"Akeem sent these. Apparently it's your birthday?"

Huh?

"That was last month." Then I realised—I wasn't Kylie anymore. "It must be Kyanna's birthday."

"Don't forget to smile when he brings the cake over later. Is Russell here?"

"Out on the terrace. Is there any news? I can't bring myself to watch the TV."

As I passed through the living room, I'd caught one tearful interview with Shane's mother on the news, the interviewer seated at a scarred wooden table in the pizza restaurant Mrs. Chapman had run alone since her husband passed on a decade ago. Even though I'd never much liked the food there, I'd often bought dinner anyway to support her. Friends should help friends, right? Or so I'd thought.

"Hashtag bike-bitch is trending on Twitter. They've found the dirt bike, but from what we've heard, they're no closer to locating you or Mimi."

"You've had over a million views on YouTube too," Russell said, appearing behind me.

Leyton gave a low whistle. "It was at eight hundred thousand when I left the office. Plus some Z-list celebrity's arguing with the road safety brigade after he said you were hot and they took offence, and Bad Boy Clothing's made you an open offer to become their spokesmodel."

Strewth. "They realise there's a warrant out for my arrest, right?"

"I'm not sure they've fully thought things through."

"Is there anything else? Or is the whole world treating this as a joke?"

Leyton's smile dropped. "I promise we're not treating this like a joke, Ky. The team's been working overnight. We've got hold of a copy of the triple-zero call reporting John's murder."

"We already tried to trace the woman, but she's a ghost."

"Ghosts don't exist. Did you find anyone else who heard the gunshot?"

"Nobody." And believe me, I'd looked. "Why don't we sit down? This isn't the sort of thing we should be discussing on the doorstep."

Russell reclaimed the spot in front of his laptops, Leyton sat opposite him, and I pulled out the chair at the end of the table. My circumstances left me reluctant to get close to anyone, no matter how fleetingly, constantly afraid that any connection would be torn to shreds by the next disaster to come my way.

Leyton opened his laptop and played the call back. It'd been years since I heard it, and the fear in the woman's voice still made my chest seize.

She kept it brief.

"I'm walking my dog on North Street, and I h-h-heard..." A pause. Rustling. "I heard, well, it sounded like a gunshot."

"Ma'am, whereabouts on North Street?"

"Farther up, s-s-somewhere near the red posting box? And I saw a man running."

I remembered the posting box—it was right in front of John's house. We'd even checked inside it for the weapons. And we'd never traced the man seen running either, so we couldn't be sure whether he was a suspect or just a jogger.

"A car's on its way. Can I take your name?"

Click.

The words took me back three years, to a time when I'd been content, when Jasper John's murder had just been one more case out of hundreds and I'd been an ambitious constable eager to make the step up to detective. I'd still had so much to learn, and Michael was meant to be my mentor. I'd been so freaking happy when I got assigned to his squad. His solve rates, his arrest record, his network of informants—they were all legendary. But hindsight was a wonderful thing, and now I could see that while he'd given me great appraisals and said nice things to my face, I'd been little more than his errand girl. He'd taught me nothing, but he'd fucked me in more ways than one.

Leyton brought me back to the present. "She sounds scared. Terrified even. But you know what she doesn't sound?"

"What?"

"Breathless. Think about it—if you were a civilian and you'd just heard a gunshot close by, wouldn't you run like hell to get out of there?"

"I guess."

"And we know she must've been bloody close. You said it was a silenced pistol you found in your kitchen? Those things don't make a lot of noise."

Right. Leyton was absolutely right. Why the hell hadn't I thought of that? Probably because Michael had been careful to distract me every time I asked difficult questions. I really hadn't been much of a detective, had I?

"Yes, it was silenced. And Jasper John's house had a thick hedge out front."

"I know—I took a look around before I came here. Our mystery woman must've been right outside when she heard the shot, not further along the street the way she implied."

"She sounded hazy about the location," Russell said. "How dark was it?"

I screwed my eyes shut, trying to remember. "Gloomy, but not pitch black. There aren't many streetlights on that stretch, and a couple of the bulbs were out."

"And what if she hid to make the call? Not everybody can run fast."

"It's a possibility," Leyton agreed. "The houses on that stretch all have front gardens. Plenty of trees and bushes for cover."

"What about the dog?" I asked. "What if it had barked?"

"What if there was no dog? She might've been in the area for another reason, one she didn't want to admit to."

"Like what?"

"A mistress visiting a lover, a thief casing a target, a hooker on her way to a client... Plenty of options. She sounded young—maybe a teenager out visiting a boyfriend she wasn't supposed to have? I'll send the recording around the office, see if anyone recognises the voice."

"We tried that before."

Unlike, say, the UK or the US, Australia didn't have much regional variation when it came to accents. We couldn't even tell if she was local to Brisbane.

"We'll keep trying. We have to—if the girl was near enough when the killer left the house, she might even be able to ID him, or at least work with a sketch artist."

My stomach twisted into knots. What if Leyton was right? What if there was a witness out there somewhere who could place Michael at the scene, but we never found her?

"What about the phone she called from?" Russell asked. "Did anyone trace that?"

We'd tried. "It was registered to a doctor from Sydney. She had no idea how her name got on the paperwork, and she had an alibi for that night."

"Which lends credence to the theory that there was something off about this witness, don't you think?" Leyton asked.

What could I do but agree? "Yes."

"We'll look for the girl, but there aren't many leads to her whereabouts, so we need to explore other avenues too."

"What avenues?"

"This 'Froggy'. He appears in some of Brenner's other messages too, and recently. Take a look at these."

I dragged my chair around the corner of the table, and Russell took the seat on the other side of Leyton. Recently? I checked the dates, and the new batch of messages had been sent on Sunday evening, less than half a day before Shane plastered himself to the side of a truck.

"How did you get those?" I asked Russell.

"Once I've got access to the account, I can see

everything, old and new."

Wow. I was never trusting an app again.

Duke916: *************************
Bossman: Why?
Duke916: *************************
Bossman: He always reckons there's heat. Froggy's a paranoid freak.
Duke916: *************************
Bossman: We're not delaying.
Duke916: *************************
Bossman: Where's he want to change it to?
Duke916: *************************
SurfsUp: *************************

Bossman: Some bloke probably looked at him funny in the dunny.

Duke916: *************************
SurfsUp: *************************

Bossman: Smokey's already out, and the rest are running low. Don't be a wuss.

SurfsUp: *************************

Bossman: We're providing a service, and the customer's fucking king. Tell Froggy it's on.

Dammit, if only we had the rest. Froggy was the one other person who might know something about what went on that night. Even if he only had an idea of Michael's state of mind at the time, it could help to build a case for my defence.

"It looks as though they were supposed to meet Froggy somewhere, and Froggy was worried about getting caught."

"Which suggests that perhaps the meeting wasn't

for entirely legal purposes," Russell said. "Filling in the blanks, it seems as if Shane was rearranging the location of the rendezvous, and Owen wasn't keen to go at all."

Leyton nodded. "And speaking of lines, Michael sure seems to cross them a lot. And he doesn't learn from his mistakes, either. John's murder was most likely designed to cover up some other crime, and yet still he carries on."

"Why would he stop?" I asked. "Nobody's ever come close to catching him. He's still the QPS's golden boy."

"Yet. Nobody's come close to catching him *yet*."

"What can we do? All we've got is one side of a conversation, and that's so vague Superintendent Clarke would never act on it."

"What about following Brenner and Mills?" Russell asked. "This meeting might not have happened yet, and even if it has, they're bound to do something else nefarious."

Nefarious... Russell was so...so posh. Three years ago, I'd have laughed at his accent and the way he used long words when short ones would do. That was partly Michael's influence—he'd had a cruel streak, I realised that now. And my time away had taught me to see the good in people who might be very different to me.

Today, Kylie 2.0 appreciated that Russell was a kind man who'd gone out of his way to help solve a problem that wasn't his to begin with. Yes, Michael, Shane, and Owen had used Ether to communicate, and I'd once been angry with Russell for creating the app, but if it didn't exist, they'd have found another way.

Scum always floats.

"Owen's paranoid about being followed," I said.

"He'd spot a tail. And Michael's an asshole, but he's not stupid."

"Then we need to take a different approach. Russell, are you sure there's no way to decrypt those other messages? Shane's in particular." Leyton pointed to a spot halfway down the conversation. "It looks as if he gave Michael a location here."

"Sorry. The only way is to physically have the phone."

"Which probably went to the morgue," I pointed out. "Shane always carried it in his jacket pocket."

"Hmmm," Leyton said.

Hmmm? "What's that supposed to mean?"

He shoved his chair back. Closed his laptop. "It means I need to go."

"Why? What's wrong?"

Leyton was already halfway to the door. "Speak soon. Enjoy the rest of your birthday."

Russell and I stared after him.

"Well, that escalated quickly. What did I say?"

"Maybe he's going to break into the morgue?"

Russell's tone said he was joking, but I feared there might be some truth in it. Not that I had a lot of hope. Even if Leyton got inside, Shane hadn't survived the crash, so what state would the phone be in?

I had no time to consider it when footsteps sounded on the terrace.

"Coo-eee. It's me."

Akeem. I groaned out loud.

"Want me to get rid of him?" Russell asked.

Russell had done too much for me already. "It's okay; I'll speak to him."

At least, I would if I could get a word in edgeways.

"Happy birthday!" Akeem held out a bottle of champagne. "Shall we open this now?"

"It's nine o'clock in the morning."

"So? It's 3 p.m. somewhere in the world. Mario's on his way with smoked salmon bagels, and Yen will be here in fifteen minutes to do a pedicure. And a manicure too, if you want." He grabbed my hand, held it up, and examined it. "Yes, definitely a manicure. I'll tell her. And then Aurelie's coming for a yoga session."

"Honestly, it's fine. I don't need—"

"You *do* need. Your toe polish is chipped."

I hadn't even wanted it in the first place, but Bradley, Emmy's assistant back in Virginia, had insisted. And now the last thing I could afford to do was risk two more people recognising me.

"I'm not so good at meeting new people. Really, I'd rather just spend today on my own. Well, with my, uh, husband."

Akeem leaned in and lowered his voice to a conspiratorial whisper. "Don't worry, I know all about your little problem. Emmy filled me in."

What? "She...she told you?"

"Yes, but I'm excellent at keeping secrets."

Just when I thought things couldn't get any worse... "Who else knows?"

"Nobody here. Just Leyton and the others at Blackwood."

"If you know I'm trying to keep a low profile, then why are you doing this?" I hissed. "I don't need freaking beauty treatments."

"Because I always spoil guests on their birthdays, and everyone would think it was weird if I ignored you. Don't worry—Mario's terrible with faces, and Yen'll be looking at your feet."

"But—"

"You don't look anything like the pictures on TV, anyway. Who did your hair back then? Because it was a crime against style. The fringe suits you so much better." He reached out and fiddled with the front of my hair, arranging it to frame my face. "You'll need your roots done soon, but I can have someone take care of that."

"Uh…"

"Ooh, here's Mario. Do you want to sit inside or out here? There's not much of a breeze, but the plumerias smell divine."

Arguing would be pointless, wouldn't it?

"Out here, I guess."

Best to enjoy the sunshine while I still could. Akeem knowing my secrets made me uncomfortable, but even though Emmy was borderline insane, I trusted her judgment when it came to people. It was far better than mine at any rate.

I caught Russell's eye through the window, and he struggled to suppress a smirk before he turned back to his laptop. Okay, I was a pushover. I'd left my backbone behind when I fled my old apartment.

"Excellent choice," Akeem said. "Mario, set the bagels out over here on the table."

CHAPTER 8 - KYLIE

MY PRETTY BLUE toenails matched the sky on Wednesday morning. Eight o'clock, and the sun was already beating down without a single puff of cloud to temper the heat.

This living-in-limbo was hard to take. I felt helpless, not to mention guilty. Everyone else was out there trying to fix my mess while I was stuck in a luxury resort getting beauty treatments. I just wanted to *do* something. Yesterday's yoga session had helped, but Aurelie made me uncomfortable. She'd looked at me just a little too closely, a little too often.

"Can you send me the rest of Michael's messages?" I'd asked Russell yesterday afternoon. Perhaps if I looked through them, something might spark an idea.

"No."

"No?"

"Leyton's going through them for clues."

"Why can't I read them too?"

He glanced up, peering over the top of those shouldn't-be-sexy glasses. "Because a number of them aren't very complimentary."

Russell was trying to protect my feelings? That was...sweet, I guess.

"I'm a big girl. I can take it."

"Yes, but you shouldn't have to."

"Look, everyone else is going out of their way to help on this, and I should play my part too, even if it makes me uncomfortable. Please, just give me the damn messages."

"I'm not going to get any peace if I don't, am I?"

I shrugged. He sighed.

"Fine." A minute later, he held out a memory stick. "The password's your mother's maiden name."

"How do you...?" I started.

Russell just stared at me.

"Actually, forget it. I don't want to know."

Half an hour later, I regretted not listening to Russell. Did that message mean what I thought it did?

"Oh, no way. No way!"

Russell's fingers stilled for a moment. "You've got to the part about the blow job?"

Fuck, fuck, fuck! "Yes."

Back in the good days, Michael had liked to make the occasional home movie. Strictly for personal use, he'd always assured me, and I'd trusted him. Truth be told, it was kind of hot watching ourselves back afterwards.

Except judging by the snippets in front of me, it very much looked as if Michael had filmed me sucking his cock, uploaded it to a porn site, then sent the link to his two best buddies afterwards. Cold dread didn't just settle in my stomach, it cannonballed into my gut from a great height.

"Now do you see why I didn't want you to read this stuff?" Russell asked.

"I don't need I-told-you-sos, okay? What if people could see my face? How many sleazes have watched me giving...giving..." I couldn't even say the words.

"I've already found it and taken it down. And no, I'm not telling you how many people viewed the clip."

Oh hell. That meant it was a lot.

"Could you recognise me?"

Russell's silence told me all I needed to know. Each time I thought this couldn't get any worse, it did. I sagged back in my chair, and he reached across the table to squeeze my hand.

"We'll fix this, Kylie. I promise we'll fix this."

"How? Michael's too smart."

"No, Michael's a cocky bastard. So far, he's been lucky, but luck only gets a man so far."

Really? Because from where I sat, it seemed as though Michael slept on a mattress of four-leafed clovers.

I forced my gaze back to the screen, and I'd soon lost count of the times Michael had called me a dumb blonde. Halfway through, he shortened it to DB to save those precious extra seconds of typing. Honestly, if I could've turned back the clock, I'd have cut off his balls while he slept, stuffed them into the blender, then gladly done the prison time for it.

But three-quarters of the way down the long, long list of ramblings, I spotted something odd.

Bossman: Demon got caught cos he's not as smart as us.

On its own, the one-liner in reply to Owen was a short and sweet hint at criminality, but if Demon was who I thought he was? That had bigger connotations.

All this time, I'd assumed Michael, Shane, and Owen were accepting bribes from criminals to turn a blind eye to their activities. A tip ignored here, a heads-up there. And I'd thought they wanted me out of the way because, after a few months on the task force, it was becoming clear that my ethics didn't jibe with theirs. Too many times, I'd pushed for a search or an arrest when Michael wasn't keen on the idea.

But Demon... The only Demon I knew of was a coke dealer in Rockhampton. His name was actually Damon, but somebody started rumours he was into Satanism and it wasn't difficult to see where the nickname came from. Rockhampton was out of our jurisdiction, but cops talked.

"Russell?"

"Mmm-hmm?"

Dammit, lose the glasses. "There's a message here about Demon."

"I saw that, but we don't know who Demon is yet."

"I think he's a drug dealer in Rockhampton. And Michael's comparing himself and Owen to him, which means...maybe...I don't know... This is crazy."

"You think Michael's dealing drugs?"

"He's a *cop*."

"That didn't seem to put him off murdering a man."

"True, but surely if he was selling drugs, I'd have noticed. Right? I mean, where was he keeping them? And how was he selling them? People would've needed to pick them up."

In Egypt, I'd lived next door to a guy who sold hash, and I'd noticed within five minutes. The clouds of smoke drifting over the wall, the super-mellow guys hanging out by the pool table in his backyard... Truth be told, I didn't have a problem with a little recreational pot use—I might even have partaken myself on occasion—but the harder stuff? That was a whole other story.

Was that why Michael had always offered to come to my place rather than the other way around? Two nights out of every three we'd spent together had been in my apartment, even though his house was bigger. Had he been hiding a mountain of coke in a freaking closet? Because who the hell would've searched *his* home?

Russell sucked in a breath. "I don't have those answers, but I'll tell Leyton."

That was it. He'd tell Leyton. Never in my life had I felt more helpless, more out of control of my own destiny. With little else to do, I scrolled through the rest of the messages and found nothing useful, but Michael appeared to be dating a redhead now. Can you guess what he called her?

Yep, DR. Oh, he of little imagination.

Dusk fell, and with darkness came candles, music, and a four-course gourmet dinner, courtesy of Akeem. Romantic, huh? Not really, since one of Russell's laptops took the third place at the table and he spent the entire meal staring at the screen rather than me. In the end, I skipped dessert and went straight to bed, wondering whether Thursday would be any better.

So far, it wasn't looking good. As I headed for the kitchen in search of caffeine, Russell scrambled for the remote and switched the TV off, but not before I caught my mum in tears on the screen. The press were harassing my parents now? Those maggots were the lowest of the low.

"Sorry," Russell said, swapping the remote in his

hand for a half-drunk mug of coffee. "I suppose at least they know you're still alive now."

"They always knew. Well, I hope so. Every so often, I sent them a postcard. I didn't sign them, obviously, but they'd have recognised my handwriting."

"Weren't you afraid someone would track you down?"

"No, because I got people to mail them from other countries."

Overseas, casual sex had become a vice of mine, a way of filling the void, and most guys were happy to do me a favour after I'd put out. I could have been anywhere from Italy to Ecuador.

Russell merely nodded. "Smart."

If I'd learned one thing during my time at the resort, it was that Russell was a man of few words. He turned back to the laptops. Well, at least this part of our "marriage" was realistic—two people sharing a house and pretty much ignoring each other. I tried reading a paperback from the shelf in the lounge, but once I'd skimmed the first few pages ten times over with no comprehension whatsoever, I admitted defeat. I was on the verge of calling Akeem to beg for sleeping pills or maybe some alcohol when Leyton stumbled onto the terrace.

Until that moment, I'd never seen him look anything but perfectly put together. What happened to his hair? It was sticking out in every direction, and his clothes were all crumpled. Was that lipstick on his face? And glitter on his shirt?

But he held up something silver in a plastic bag, grinning triumphantly before he collapsed onto a sun lounger.

"Got it!"

"Bloody hell," Russell said, peering out of the door. "What happened to you? Did a bust go wrong?"

"Is that a phone?" I asked.

"Shane's phone. It's battered, but it still turns on."

Holy shit. Suddenly, I was wide awake. "You're serious? How did you get it?"

"It's a long story, and I need coffee first. Preferably by intravenous drip."

"I'll make it."

Russell had already disappeared inside, clutching Leyton's prize, and I soon heard his keyboard clacking away. My foot tapped in time, impatient, as I waited for the hideously complicated coffee machine to work its magic.

Finally, I had a passable cappuccino for me, a plain black coffee for Russell, and a double espresso for Leyton, who was lying flat out with a hand over his eyes.

"I'm not sure whether you need this or sleep," I said, passing him the cup. Despite sleeping myself for eight hours last night, I'd had nightmares of the bike chase, of my brush with death at Mimi's dainty hands, and I felt like he looked.

"Both. I need both."

"What happened?"

Leyton covered his mouth while he yawned. Groaned. "So I kind of know the morgue attendant. And by 'kind of know,' I mean she hits on me every time I attend an autopsy or go to speak with the ME. So I figured I might be able to do some sort of deal to get Shane's phone, assuming his family hadn't claimed it yet."

"And you obviously did."

"Whatever's in those messages better be worth it."

"Worth what?"

"Going as Glinda's date to her grandmother's seventy-fifth birthday party."

A snort escaped. "Sounds like a riot."

"I'd rather have gone to a riot. After a couple of margaritas, she told me she wasn't wearing any underwear."

"Glinda or her grandma?"

Leyton's eyes widened in horror, and boy were they bloodshot. "Glinda, thank fuck. I figured it'd be easy—you know, drink tea, eat some cake, call an ambulance if anyone's heart gave out—but those women are wild. Glinda passed out at midnight but her grandma's crew kept going. They were teaching me to salsa dance at four o'clock this morning, and I'm not sure what happened after that, but I woke up face down on a sofa."

"Couldn't you have snuck out early?"

"Glinda thought of that—she wouldn't give me the phone until after I'd done my duty, which meant another visit to the morgue before I came here. I nearly flaked out in one of those metal drawers."

Leyton looked offended when I laughed, but I needed that moment of relief on an otherwise dark day. The stress was getting to me, Michael's reach like a boa constrictor that coiled tighter and tighter around my chest every time I took a breath.

Hold it together, Kylie. I stared past Leyton and homed in on Russell sitting at the dining table, calm and focused as his fingers worked their magic. He may not have had much to say, but his composure helped to anchor me in the storm.

"Do you need to take the phone back?"

"Nah, I got one of the interns to find a lookalike and smash it up properly. Swapped the two over."

I glanced across at Russell again. Leyton had come through with the evidence, but the question was, where would it lead?

Chapter 9 - Kylie

FOR THE THIRD time, I dragged a chair next to Russell as he did his Ether trick. The actual process was quite quick, and I leaned in, elbows on the table as I stared at the screen. Our thighs touched, my bare skin to his chinos, and I should have moved back, but I didn't. Russell kept me grounded, and I was starting to like that feeling. He didn't move either.

His fingers reminded me of a concert pianist's. Long, smooth, elegant, the way they danced over the keys. Controlled. Mesmerising. What else could he do with them?

Fuck. I should *not* have been thinking that way.

Then Shane's messages appeared on the scene, and I leaned forward, my breath hitching, everything else forgotten as I read the missing pieces of his and Michael's conversation.

Duke916: Froggy wants to change the handover point for Saturday.
Bossman: Why?
Duke916: Reckons there's heat.
Bossman: He always reckons there's heat. Froggy's a paranoid freak.
Duke916: He wants to delay too.
Bossman: We're not delaying.

Duke916: What'll I tell him?

Bossman: Where's he want to change it to?

Duke916: 39 Nabarra Street

*SurfsUp: *********************

Bossman: Some bloke probably looked at him funny in the dunny.

Duke916: You a poet now?

*SurfsUp: *********************

Bossman: Smokey's already out, and the rest are running low. Don't be a wuss.

*SurfsUp: *********************

Bossman: We're providing a service, and the customer's fucking king. Tell Froggy it's on.

The address. We had the address!

"Nabarra Street?" I'd been expecting something seedier. A warehouse or a bar, maybe, not a building on a residential street in one of the city's nicer neighbourhoods. "That's a good area."

"It's a house," Russell said, already zooming in on a satellite map.

This was no crack den, or a drug lord's mansion either. Number thirty-nine was a boxy detached home with an SUV parked on the driveway and a small swimming pool in the backyard.

"Looks kind of average."

"I'll try to find out who owns it. We should wake Leyton."

Despite the breakthrough, he was snoring softly on the sun lounger, one arm trailing on the ground. His coffee sat untouched on the table next to him. Who knew salsa-dancing seniors could tire a man out like that?

"I'll do it."

Leyton reported the news to Blackwood, then promptly closed his eyes again. Three breaths later, he was snoring, and I shifted one of the big umbrellas so he was in the shade. The last thing we needed was a lead investigator with a bad case of sunburn.

Now what? In the old days, I'd have taken a drive to Nabarra Street and had a look around. Talked to the neighbours. Watched the place to see who came and went. But in my new life, that was all out of my hands, and the frustration at being completely helpless made me want to scream.

"Is there anything I can do?" I asked Russell.

"Nope." He didn't even look up. "All in hand."

I tried yoga, but I couldn't focus. Tai had messaged me last night to see how I was, and since it was late evening in Virginia and I didn't want to distract her from doing who knew what with Ren, I typed out a reply telling her everything was going as well as expected.

Which was to say, badly.

I couldn't take another day on the sofa, so I walked down to the beach, stripping off clothing as I went. Years had passed since I swam in the ocean, and I'd missed the feel of the saltwater lapping at my feet. As I waded in deeper, the blue called to me, and it was tempting to float out to sea and never return. *But then he'd win*, I reminded myself. *Michael would win.*

I started swimming instead.

Every limb ached as I staggered up the path from the

beach. My legs felt like lead, my arms like silly string. I'd swum for over an hour along the coast, stopping halfway to float on my back and stare up at the sky while I enjoyed a few moments of peace. Of freedom. How much longer would it last?

A forty-something woman walking in the opposite direction gave me a dirty look and tugged her husband out of my way. What? Did she think exhaustion was contagious? Since she'd chosen to wear make-up to the beach, exercise was probably a foreign concept to her. What did she do to keep her figure? Rely on gourmet salads, fancy massages, and the occasional nip and tuck? Her snooty attitude was yet another reminder of how out-of-place I felt. The Black Diamond Resort wasn't my world. I was more of a hostel-and-a-barbie kind of girl. People paid thousands of dollars to stay at the Black Diamond, but I'd have given my soul to be back in my old apartment, working at my old job, with Michael nothing but a nasty dream that vanished when the sun rose.

I'd reached the edge of the terrace when a shout jarred me out of my thoughts. I couldn't make out the words, but I recognised the voice. Russell. My feet broke into a run before I'd had time to fully process things.

Leyton was only halfway off the sun lounger when I bolted past.

"What's wrong?" I asked as I skidded into the villa.

Russell had sounded upset, but he didn't look upset. His brown eyes gleamed, and he picked me up and swung me around in one smooth move, grinning.

"Nothing's wrong. I've found him!"

"Found who?"

"Froggy."

Russell still had a hold of me, and there was a moment of awkwardness when he realised that and loosened his grip. I slithered down his body, soaking him in the process since I hadn't taken a towel to the beach with me. His damp shirt clung to his body, outlining muscles that he sure didn't get from computer programming.

"Sorry," we both said in unison.

But neither of us let go entirely. No, we stood there, frozen, my hands gripping his biceps and his arms around my waist, and a flash of heat travelled south.

What was wrong with me? I couldn't have feelings for any man, let alone Russell. My world was quicksand, and if he got too close, he'd get sucked into the mire as well. Right now, he was helping me, and I couldn't afford to jeopardise that by letting my stupid heart run wild.

I needed him, but not in that way. I needed his calmness under pressure and his bravery when the chips were down. If he hadn't kept his head and reacted the way he did during that motorcycle chase, it would have been me lying cold in the morgue and not Shane. And Russell was easy to be around. Not pushy the way Michael had always been—there was no "my way or the highway." Russell gave me space. Sometimes too much space, but that was better than none at all. We'd only been sharing the villa for a few days, but I'd grown to appreciate his company, and I hoped he felt the same.

Except the way he was looking at me...

"Sorry to interrupt your moment," Leyton said. "But did you say you'd found Froggy?"

Russell's arms dropped away, and the moment was

lost.

"Uh, yes. I'm ninety-nine percent certain. The last of the pieces of the puzzle just slotted into place."

"So who is he?"

"Francis Mulhearn, also known as Dr. Feelgood."

"Mulhearn?" I said. "I'd half expected him to be French."

An ethnic slur from Michael wouldn't have surprised me in the slightest, not after everything else he'd done.

"No, he's Australian. A Sydney native. His great-grandfather moved here from Ireland at the beginning of the last century. A priest, as was Francis's father and his grandfather before him. Francis is the first of the Mulhearns to diversify away from the family business."

"How on earth did you find that out? Hacking?"

"No, it's all on his website. Once I worked out who he was, it was easy to fill in the gaps."

Russell took a seat again and clicked a couple of keys. A picture of a man appeared, brown hair, weak chin, nondescript apart from his protruding eyes. He looked like someone had grabbed him around the throat and squeezed. Frog eyes, which explained the nickname. In the background, a small plane gleamed in the sun. *Fly with Francis*, the banner at the top of the page read.

"Is the plane his?"

Russell nodded. "He offers sightseeing tours and private charters."

"I don't understand—how is he connected to Michael? And why's he called Dr. Feelgood?"

"Because he sells drugs. Coke mainly, but he can get anything for a price. His store's called Dr. Feelgood's

Emporium, and it's basically an A to Z of illegal substances. Payment's in Bitcoin or a dozen other cryptocurrencies."

Holy fuck. I felt sick. Leyton grabbed a chair and shoved it under my ass right before my legs gave way. *Drugs*. When I suggested the idea yesterday, I hadn't truly believed it myself, but now... *Drugs*? Michael wasn't just a cop, he ran the anti-drugs freaking task force, a role that put him in the perfect position to cover up his own crimes as well as other people's. But how did it all fit together?

"He has a *store*?" Leyton asked.

"On the dark web."

"The internet? But how do people get the stuff? Surely he can't mail it out like Amazon?"

"Nope. It gets delivered by couriers, like an illegal version of Just Eat. And if Michael Brenner's picking up goods from Mulhearn, I'll wager he's involved in the Brisbane network somehow."

Leyton was wide awake now, his eyes gleaming. "Fuck. If what you say is true, this is far bigger than three rogue cops."

"Yes, it is."

"What now?" I asked. "What do we do now? I mean, we've got to tell Superintendent Clarke, haven't we?"

The two men both stared at me, but Leyton was the first to laugh. "No, Ky, we do not tell Superintendent Clarke. Mimi's been asking around, and the last time someone shopped one of his people, he trod softly-softly because 'a man has to be allowed to defend himself.' Clarke gave the guy enough of a heads-up that he was able to bury the evidence."

"What did the guy do?"

"Accepted freebies from hookers. By the time the Internal Investigations Group got involved, the cop in question had talked to all the women and got them to swear they'd been on bona fide dates."

I didn't need to be a genius to work out the implications of that. Task Force Titan was the jewel in the crown of the Tactical Crime Squad, Michael its most decorated officer. Losing him, especially to a scandal, would *not* reflect well on Superintendent Clarke. I felt as if I was drowning. Drowning in my own blood because how the hell was this ever going to end well?

"What alternatives are there?" Russell asked. "He can't get away with this, surely?"

Leyton shook his head. "He won't, but I need to have a think about this and talk to some people. Can you send me whatever evidence you've collected?"

"On the condition that you don't tell anyone where it came from."

"That's a given. Where's the coffee?" Leyton spied a mug on the table, picked it up, and made a face as he drank the contents cold. "I need to get back to the office. Look after Ky, okay?"

"I don't need to be reminded to do that."

Why did my heart skip a beat at his words?

Chapter 10 - Kylie

I EXPECTED RUSSELL to settle in behind his laptops again, but he surprised me by closing the lids. All of them. *Clack. Clack. Clack.*

"So, what do you want to do this afternoon?" he asked.

"Huh? Don't you have to work?"

"I think I've done as much as I can on your case for now. We know who Michael's planning to meet, and we know where. The next step is in Blackwood's hands. Leyton'll call if he needs me for anything else."

"What about your regular job?"

"Don't tempt me. For the first time in my life, I've tried delegating, and I'm already getting twitchy." He took a step closer. "And I've been neglecting you. Six days, we've been here, and we've barely spoken."

"Just like a real married couple," I kidded.

"Kylie... Let's do something fun today."

"Like what? I can't go out anywhere."

"We'll be fine if we're careful. Everyone's looking for a blonde woman skulking around on her own, not a brunette on a date with her husband. You don't even look like the pictures on TV, and we've got rings and everything."

Should I risk it? I was going stir crazy in the villa, and who knew how much longer I'd be free? The clock was ticking in the back of my mind, counting down to the moment when I'd either get caught or have to run again. Just for one day, couldn't I pretend to be normal?

"What do you suggest?"

"Where's that brochure?"

"What brochure?"

"The hotel guide with the activities in it." He headed for the desk on the other side of the living room. The bottom two drawers of the pedestal were locked—I'd checked them right after we arrived—but the top one contained an assortment of guide books. "Here it is. How about going to the spa? They do some sort of couples thing. Uh, what's an Oxygenerio facial?"

"I have no idea, but I don't want people looking at my face."

"A boat trip? Do you know how to sail?"

"Nuh-uh. You?"

"Yes, but on second thoughts..." He glanced outside. "There's not much wind."

"We could go snorkelling?"

Russell shuddered. "What about sharks?"

"They're rare. I swam for an hour this morning, and I'm still alive."

"You swam in the *ocean*? I thought you went to the pool."

"I love swimming in the ocean."

I loved to scuba dive too, and once you'd seen what was under the water, it wasn't so scary anymore. Every few months, when we'd saved up enough money and had a few days off, Chloe and I would pile into her old Holden and head up the coast to Rockhampton, taking it in turns to drive. Just us, our bathers and towels, and the old battery-powered radio that sat in the passenger footwell because the car stereo was broken. Life had been so much simpler back then.

"How about golf?" Russell suggested. "They've got an eighteen-hole course."

"Golf? That's just for old rich posh people."

He did that looking-over-his-glasses thing again, and I swallowed down a groan.

"Uh, you play golf, don't you?"

"At school, I was captain of the golf team."

"Your school had a golf team?"

"We did. We got the choice of either golf or rugby, and I figured there was less chance of breaking my nose playing golf."

"I'm sorry I said you were old and posh and rich."

"Well, I guess I'm two out of the three. So, what do you say? Golf?"

"I don't know the first thing about it."

"I can teach you."

"What about clubs? Balls?"

"I'm sure Akeem can help out there."

Of course Akeem could. Half an hour later, I found myself standing beside Russell at the first hole, dressed in a polo shirt, smart cropped trousers, spiked shoes, and a sun visor. What had Akeem done? Raided the club shop? Russell had suitable clothes of his own, and he insisted on carrying our bag of borrowed clubs too.

"Can't we rent one of those buggy things?"

"That's cheating. Golf's good exercise if you carry the bag, and goodness knows, I need it with the amount of time I spend sitting at my computer."

"You don't look like a desk jockey."

"Five years ago, I did. I was three stone overweight

and living on junk food when the button popped off the last pair of trousers I owned that still did up, and I decided I'd had enough."

"No way. You were overweight? But you're so hot." Oh shit! *Think before you open your big, stupid mouth, Kylie.* "Sorry, I shouldn't have said that. Totally inappropriate."

Russell turned away to rummage through the bag of golf clubs. He selected one, drew it out, and straightened.

"Your honesty's refreshing, Mrs. Watson." Was that a hint of a smile? "Let's start with a 3-wood for this hole."

Before I could sink into the ground, we were interrupted by a grey-haired couple. The woman looked me up and down then glared at her husband when he did the same.

"Are you about to tee off?" he asked.

"Why don't you go first?" Russell said, wrapping one arm around my waist. "We're in no hurry, are we, darling?"

Darling? Oh, right, that was me. "No, you go ahead."

"That's mighty kind of you. Are you here on your honeymoon?"

I stiffened, but Russell just smiled. Despite the years I'd spent faking everything from undercover drug buys to orgasms to my entire life, Russell was clearly the professional in this situation. Why was I so off-balance? It was the lack of practice, right? The month off in Virginia? Nothing whatsoever to do with the man standing beside me, no way.

"We've been married for four years now." He drew

me closer, kissed my hair. "But when you meet the right person, every day's a honeymoon, isn't it?"

"Gerald, will you hurry up?"

"I wouldn't know," the man muttered under his breath. "Coming, sweetheart."

The couple each gave their balls a hard *thwack*, then ambled off after them. Two caddies trailed behind, carrying their bags, and once again, I was reminded of how the other half lived.

"So what do I do?" I asked Russell. "I've only ever played minigolf before, and even then I missed every time."

Russell explained how to set up the ball on the tee, how to hold the club, and how to drive the ball far into the distance. At least, I thought he did. I kept getting distracted by that ass in those fancy trousers, which meant I missed most of what he said.

Finally, it was my turn. I lined up the ball, grabbed the club, and swung it as hard as I could. A bloody great lump of grass flew up into the air and landed at Russell's feet. The ball stayed exactly where I'd placed it.

"Ah, shit."

Russell tried and failed to keep a straight face. "I think there are some small improvements to be made. Do you mind?"

"Mind what?"

Gently, hesitantly, he moved my hands closer together on the club. Adjusted my feet. Straightened my body and lined me up next to the ball. Little shivers ran through me everywhere he touched, which was dumb because he was basically acting as a freaking golf instructor. Had deprivation of human company sent me that crazy?

"There, now try."

Thwack. "Yee-hah! I did it! Uh, where did it go?"

Russell had his hand above his eyes to block the sun as he peered into the distance. "You probably don't want to know. Why don't you try another one? I won't tell."

Six attempts later, I managed to get a ball to stay on the green stuff as opposed to vanishing into the trees.

"Good. Off we go."

Russell held out a hand, and I looked around to see who was watching. The older couple had long-since disappeared, but a group was heading our way from the clubhouse. Well spotted. I slipped my hand into his.

"Do you play golf often?" I asked as we walked.

"Once a week, usually. I took a break for a couple of years after school, and that was when the middle-aged spread started early. Now I'm more strict with myself—no more than three hours straight in the chair on a normal day, and then I have to take a break. For a while, I had a personal trainer, but then I installed a home gym, and I use that at least five times a week."

"You didn't move for eight hours yesterday."

"These are far from normal days, Kylie. Is that your ball over there?"

Yes, yes it was, and it took me three more clubs and seventeen whacks and taps to get it into the hole. Russell did it in three and spent the rest of the time checking his phone. What happened to delegating? But I succeeded nonetheless, so that was something to be happy about, right?

"That's better," Russell said. "A smile."

"This is frustrating, but not as boring as I thought

it'd be."

"It gets better, honestly. Next hole?"

"Yup."

"Much as I hate to admit it, my mother was right about one thing when she convinced me to go to Egypt —I do need to have more fun. I see that now."

"What are you gonna do after this?"

"After golf?"

"No, after you leave Australia. Will you go back to London?"

"I haven't thought that far ahead. I need to attend board meetings once a month, but I can do some of those by phone, and I can work from anywhere. How about you?"

"Me what?"

"What will you do?"

"At the moment, it's looking like a choice of jail or China. Maybe Morocco if I can get a flight there."

"Don't talk like that. We're so close to catching Michael."

"But even if we do catch him, how does that clear me? Unless he admits he set me up, it doesn't. And I can tell you now that Michael will *never* admit to that. He'll go to the grave with his secrets."

I may have been so very wrong about him in the past, but that was one thing I was certain of. Michael would be an asshole to the last. It was ingrained in his character, a stain on his soul.

Russell gave me a side hug, and having his arm around me no longer felt strange the way it once did. I leaned into him and rested my head on his shoulder. How much more time would I have him around?

"Forget Michael this afternoon," he said. "Focus on

re-landscaping Emmy's golf course instead."

A hiccup of laughter escaped because I *had* left a lot of craters. "She'd go mental if she could see me."

"I don't think so. Akeem told me she's not so good at golf either."

"Really?"

"Apparently, she knows enough to bluff her way through the occasional game with dignitaries, but she mostly just cheats."

"No way."

"Yes way. Half the guys at school used to cheat too. Getting into practice for their future careers as politicians, I guess."

"You never got tempted?"

"I found it far more satisfying to pretend that the ball was the science teacher's head. Hit that sucker every time. I can still hear his voice now—*Russell Weisz, you've got mitosis and meiosis mixed up* again. *I think a detention's in order, don't you*?"

"You weren't a big fan of biology, then?"

Russell threw me a glance over his shoulder, and for an instant, his eyes darkened. "Oh, I mastered the parts that matter."

What? What was that supposed to mean? I hurried to catch up as Russell strode towards the next hole, his hand outstretched for me to take. What parts? What parts had he mastered? Was he talking about—

"Coo-eee!"

I spun to see Akeem coming towards us, bouncing over the grass in a golf cart. Had something happened? Russell gripped my hand tighter.

"What's wrong?" he asked.

"It's hot, you've got through six holes, and nobody's

offered you any refreshments." Akeem stopped the cart in front of us, blocking our way. "It's important to keep your energy up, so I've brought drinks and snacks."

On any other golf course in the world, drinks and snacks probably meant a bottle of water and maybe a packet of peanuts, but we were on Emmy's golf course, and this was Akeem. Two minutes later, he'd set up a table complete with a spotless white tablecloth and set out a bottle of champagne in an ice bucket plus a selection of canapés.

"Is this wise?" I asked. I was quite bad enough at golf already without adding alcohol into the mix.

"Why wait until the nineteenth hole? Let your hair down."

Oh, screw it. There was no champagne in prison, and if I fell over, Akeem could pick us up in the cart later. Who knew, perhaps the alcohol would even improve my aim? When Akeem waved us off to the seventh hole, I had a pleasant buzz on.

"I think I like golf now," I said as I stumbled into Russell. "This is fun."

He muttered something that sounded suspiciously like "Heaven help me" then mustered up a smile. "I'm glad you're enjoying yourself."

"Isn't this better than typing?"

"Typing. Yes. Kylie, the green's this way."

Six more holes, and Akeem reappeared, this time with cocktails for me, beer for Russell, crustless sandwiches, and bags of fancy hand-cooked crisps. Was this really what rich people did all day? Played drunk golf? No wonder so many terrible business deals got done on the golf course. Russell had taken four business-y phone calls, and I had no idea how he managed to speak without slurring.

"I'm getting better at this, huh?" I said as I smacked the ball into the air at the fifteenth hole. "Aw, it went in the sand again."

I climbed down to try and hit it out, but I fell on my ass instead, and when Russell attempted to help me up, I accidentally pulled him into the sandpit as well. Oops.

"Sorry."

"I think it's time we headed back, don't you?"

"What about the rest of the holes?"

"We can finish those another day."

"Okay." I lay back in the sand and reached my arms over my head, stretching out. "Why don't we just stay here? It's like lying on the beach, except with grass instead of water."

Russell lay down next to me, propped up on one elbow, and I thought he might be pissed. But when I managed to focus, I saw mirth in his eyes rather than anger. Michael would've been annoyed for sure. He'd always hated when I got drunk, even though it was usually him who kept plying me with alcohol.

"At least there aren't any sharks," Russell said.

"Nope. No sharks on land. Just snakes."

"Snakes?" He scrambled to his knees, looking wildly around. "Where?"

I got the giggles, then wished I hadn't because I felt a tiny bit sick. "Just relax. They mostly keep away from humans. It's only if you scare them that they bite."

"I think I should call Akeem to pick us up. It's time we both had some dinner."

"Chicken."

"Hey, it's only natural to be nervous of snakes. A lot of them are poisonous."

"No, I want chicken. That thing on the room service menu with the chicken and the asparagus." I held my hands up. "Don't go. I'll protect you from the snakes, I promise."

Russell lay back down beside me, a little gingerly it seemed. "I'm sure I can arrange asparagus-stuffed chicken."

"I always wanted to be able to cook, but I can't. Can you cook?"

"My mother always told me a gentleman should be able to make at least one good meal."

"And what meal can you make?"

"Beef Wellington, spaghetti bolognese, and lobster thermidor."

"That's three meals. You're such an over-achiever."

"Guess I am."

"Did your mother teach you to make them?"

"Goodness, no. Her chef did. Mother doesn't get her hands dirty in the kitchen."

"We come from different worlds, you and me."

"But right now, we're living in the same one, so let's make the most of it." He fished around in his pocket for his phone. "Akeem, could you please pick us up? ... No, we're at the fifteenth hole. ... Uh, no, we're lying in a bunker. ... Yes, lying in a bunker. It's perhaps best not to ask." Russell shook his head as he hung up, seemingly unable to believe the situation himself. "He'll be here in five minutes. Try to stay awake, okay?"

"Yup, absolutely."

I didn't manage it. I was vaguely aware of Russell hauling me out of the sandpit and laying me across the back seat of the golf cart, then holding me in place as we headed for Emmy's villa. That solid thigh under my head... Mmm... I came to as he carried me into the bedroom, and when I opened my eyes, our lips were just inches apart. Alcohol took over, and I leaned in, only for him to move out of reach.

"I'm not doing this while you're drunk."

Instead, I got the soft press of his lips to my forehead once he'd laid me on the bed and tucked me under the quilt. Then he smoothed the hair away from my face and dimmed the light.

"Goodnight, Kylie."

The door clicked behind him.

CHAPTER 11 - KYLIE

REGRETS? I HAD a hundred of them, but none so much as when I woke the next morning with a mob of kangaroos jumping around in my skull. How much wine had I drunk? It must've been at least half the bottle, plus those cocktails, and I was such a lightweight. Michael used to tease me about it, the way I couldn't hold my drink, but that still didn't stop him from taking advantage.

I'd been under the influence on our first night together, inebriated at a colleague's leaving party in an effort to prove I was one of the guys and still tipsy when Michael drove me home. He'd kissed me on the doorstep, and my alcohol-addled brain had been weirdly flattered. Flattered that he wanted me—*me*—when women had been throwing themselves at him all night. We ended up in my bed, where he came and I didn't. That pretty much summed up our whole relationship. Looking back, I could see it was all about him.

Why did I go along with it? Because I was young and I didn't know any better. I'd been dazzled, blinded by his freaking aura. Women walked into walls over Michael. Flirted with him in front of me. I guess I thought that if so many other girls wanted him, then he must've been a real catch. That he was as good as it got.

I'd been wrong. So very fucking wrong. I'd had enough of alpha males to last me a lifetime. Give me a beta any day.

That had been my strategy as I travelled. I'd gone for the shy men. The quiet ones. Always tourists, and never anyone whose flight home was more than a day away. I didn't want deep and meaningful, just a fleeting connection. Enough to ward off the loneliness for another week or two. Nights of fumbling and bad sex because if I'd suggested an evening of cuddling and a movie, any sane man would have run a mile.

And it had worked. I'd kept my emotions in check, even felt the odd spark of happiness as my life in Australia had faded into history. Except then it fell apart. One day in Egypt, the life I'd constructed, the walls I'd built around myself, they all got smashed down. And now here I was.

With the ultimate fucking beta.

How much of a fool had I made of myself yesterday? I screwed my eyes shut, trying to remember, but all I got was fuzz.

Fuzz followed by a soft knock at the door.

"Kylie?"

"I'm awake." It came out as a croak, and I peeped under the covers. Yep, awake and still wearing golf clothes. How nasty did my breath smell?

Even if it stank, there was nothing I could do about it because the door creaked open. Russell was carrying a cup and saucer and wearing those damned glasses again. Too late, the memories of last night came back. The way I'd attempted to do something utterly stupid, and his words afterwards. *I'm not doing this while you're drunk.*

"Peppermint tea. I know there's no scientific evidence, but I found it helped my hangovers when I was at school."

Once again, I could've kissed him. No, really. I realised at that moment I was in big trouble.

"Thanks."

"Leyton's coming by in half an hour, or I'd have let you sleep. Can I get you anything else? Coffee? Some breakfast?"

Just a do-over of yesterday afternoon. I shook my head, then regretted it because my flipping brain hurt. "Russell, I'm really sorry I drank too much yesterday. I've barely touched alcohol since I left here the first time, and it hit me a lot harder than I thought it would."

"Nothing to be sorry for. I haven't had that much fun playing golf in years."

Great, now I was a laughingstock. "I stink at it."

"The first time I played, it took me twelve hours to get around the course, and I hit seven balls into a lake. You'll get better, but perhaps we should sunbathe on the beach instead of in a bunker next time?"

"Good idea. I doubt they'll let me back on the golf course anyway. Did I make a complete fool of myself?"

"Uh...no."

He hesitated too long.

"Now tell me the truth."

It couldn't be as bad as the blow job video. *Nothing* could be as bad as the blow job video.

"While you were, er, resting, a lady hit a ball a foot from your head, then nearly had a heart attack when she came to retrieve it. She thought she'd knocked you out, and Akeem had to drive her back to the clubhouse."

"Oh, crap. I should apologise to her, maybe get her some flowers or something."

"Already taken care of. Her husband saw the funny side." Russell reached out to brush a stray hair away from my eyes. "I'll leave you to take a shower."

Why did he have to be so fucking *nice*?

As the steaming water cascaded over my shoulders, I cursed Michael, Superintendent Clarke, and the universe in general for putting me into this position. Fantasy versus reality. Heaven versus hell. Every day I spent with Russell, I grew to understand him better, and with that understanding came an impossible longing, an ache that started deep in my chest and threatened to consume all rational thought if I let it.

Why did I have to meet the right man at the wrong time? Fate? Although if I hadn't been on the run, our paths would never have crossed, would they? If Michael hadn't been the world's biggest shithead, perhaps he and I would still have been together, and maybe I'd even have been happy, not knowing that there was anything better out there.

Ten minutes passed, twenty, and I forced myself to turn off the water and get dressed. I had to face Leyton, and Russell, and... Oh. Mimi.

"Sorry. I overslept a bit, and..."

"No worries," Leyton said. "We've just come to fill you in on what's happening."

"And?" The word tumbled out.

"The team had a long discussion yesterday evening, and we've decided to get the Feds involved."

"The Feds?"

Didn't he think there were enough law enforcement

officers sniffing around already?

"It's the best option. Blackwood could carry out the raid, but we can't tie the mess up afterwards and get it through the courts without assistance. We've got contacts in the Federal Police, and they're keeping this hush-hush."

"Superintendent Clarke doesn't know?"

"Not a word."

"He's already under investigation for poor results," Mimi said. "Do this right, and he'll go down along with the rest of them."

"But what about me?"

"That's phase two. If Michael's been dabbling in the drugs trade, then he's most likely got money stashed away. While the raid's happening, Mimi's gonna take a look around his place to see if we can find his nest egg. Russell, can you be on standby to go through his computer?"

"Of course."

"Michael still lives in the same house as he did three years ago. Ky, can you talk us through what you remember about it? The layout, security, possible hiding places, anything that might be useful. It could have changed, but it'll be a start."

I thought they'd just want a few diagrams, but they interrogated me for two hours. First, I described the obvious—the hollowed-out book where he kept his passport, the spare key to the shed hidden under a rock by the swimming pool, the attic he rarely used—but as Leyton continued with his questioning, I recalled things I barely even knew in the first place. The creaky floorboard in the upstairs hallway. The way the back door lock stuck until you jiggled it a bit.

And the experience left me drained. Twenty-seven years old, and I needed an afternoon nap.

"Tired?" Russell asked after Leyton and Mimi left.

"Exhausted."

"Why don't you get some rest until it's time to cook dinner? I'll catch up on a bit of work."

"*Cook* dinner?"

"I thought you wanted to learn? And I can make beef Wellington, so..."

Oh, hell. I was done for. Russell was so sweet it hurt, and I tried to smile even as my eyes prickled.

"Cooking sounds great." I turned away before he saw my tears. "Absolutely perfect."

CHAPTER 12 - KYLIE

"DO YOU WANT the good news or the bad news?" Russell asked when I shuffled out of my bedroom at— what time was it? The monstrosity on the wall said six o'clock.

"Please, no more bad news."

"Okay, the good news first. Emmy emailed. Remember Maury Devlin and Anton de Bellis?"

With all the horrors in Australia, Devlin and de Bellis had faded to the far recesses of my mind, but now they popped forward, front and centre. Devlin was an art dealer from Yonkers and a cog in the smuggling ring we'd helped to bust in Egypt. De Bellis was one of his buyers.

"Yes, I remember them."

"They both got arrested yesterday. Dawn raids, one in New York and one in Switzerland. The pair of them are in jail, and the police are going through their art collections for stolen goods."

Finally, some justice had been served, even if it wasn't against Michael. "That's great! So, uh, what's the bad news?"

"Akeem somehow heard about it and sent this..." Russell reached over to the fridge and pulled out a bottle of pink champagne. "Apparently, it's to help us celebrate."

"What, he doesn't think I got drunk enough yesterday?"

"I thought that might be your reaction."

"I'm never touching alcohol again."

"I thought that too, so I asked the chef to make us a nice dessert instead." Russell grimaced slightly. "Which unfortunately turned out to be champagne mousse with sangria sorbet. How do you feel about cheese and biscuits?"

"I'm good with cheese and biscuits."

And I was good with him showing me how to roast the beef and fry the mushrooms and wrap the whole lot in prosciutto and pastry to bake. Like yesterday with golf, he had a way of manhandling me around the kitchen, gently and with the lightest of touches. By the time the vegetables went in to roast, I needed to concertina myself into the ice bucket to cool off.

How was this man still single? When we first met, he mentioned that he'd split up with a girlfriend before he travelled to Egypt, and honestly, the woman must have lost her mind.

"I feel as though I should dress up for this dinner," I said in an attempt to steer my dirty mind back to cleaner territory.

"Really? I was thinking the opposite. This won't be ready for half an hour, and the pool's right there. Want to cool off?"

More than he could ever know. I nodded before I'd fully thought the situation through, only for flames to lick up my insides when Russell pulled off his polo shirt and headed for the terrace. Oh, crap.

Don't drool, Kylie. "I, uh, just need to change into my bathers."

And maybe take a cold shower while I was at it. Someone up there hated me.

Hated me enough to send me back out to the swimming pool in a bikini and make me sit there for thirty minutes talking to a man who seemed genuinely interested in having a conversation as opposed to staring at my boobs.

Why? Why? Why?

Even when he put his shirt back on and I covered up with a filmy sundress that came courtesy of Bradley, my stupid hormones didn't let up. And worse, the food tasted as good as it looked. With each mouthful, I stewed over every moment I'd spent with Russell, from the time in Egypt to our occasional meetings at Riverley to the disastrous golf outing to his words last night.

"Are you okay?" he asked when I dropped my fork on my empty plate. "You've gone quiet."

"Just thinking."

If Michael had been sitting opposite, I'd have gotten a snarky, "Dare I ask?" But this was Russell.

"Want to talk about it?"

Not really, but I had to because otherwise I'd never know. And the not knowing was eating me up inside.

"Last night, when you carried me to bed..."

His phone buzzed, and he glanced down at it. Normally, I hated the way the stupid thing stole his attention, but at that particular second, I was grateful for the lack of eye contact.

"Yes?"

"We were kinda close, and you said you wouldn't do anything when I was drunk."

"Of course not. I'd never take advantage of a

woman."

"Would you have done something if I wasn't drunk?"

Now I had his attention. He peered at me over the top of his glasses, and all my blood ran south.

"Yes."

Yes. A simple, honest answer I hadn't truly been expecting.

But what should I do about it?

Slowly, deliberately, I pushed our plates and glasses to the side. Leaned across the table propped up on my elbows, never breaking eye contact with him. It was as if the devil herself had taken over, and I was just along for the ride.

"I'm not drunk now."

The bloody phone buzzed again, so I picked it up and tossed it into the swimming pool.

"What the—" Russell started.

"It's waterproof. It'll still be there in half an hour."

He stared at the phone as it sank, then slowly turned back to me. Now what? Was he angry? He looked kind of intense. My heart thumped against my ribcage, threatening to break its way out. What had I done?

"Sorry," I mumbled.

After the briefest hesitation, he hooked his hands under my armpits and dragged me right over the damn table.

"You think this is going to be over in half an hour, Kylie?"

Oh, holy mother of hotness. Those eyes had gone from coppery brown to dark to fiery, and now it was my turn to stare after the phone.

"Uh, then perhaps you should—"

"I've got a spare," he said. Then he kissed me, and I discovered yet another hidden side to Russell Weisz. What the hell had those nuns taught him at boarding school?

My toes curled into my thongs as his tongue parted my lips, and I had to clutch at his shoulders to keep my balance. He soon adjusted his grip, wrapping his arms around me, his hands gathering the colourful beach cover-up Bradley had insisted I bring even though I thought it was too bright.

Russell paused as if to ask me if this was okay, and I moaned an unintelligible "yes" into his mouth. Fortunately, he understood, and those hands cupped my butt cheeks, sliding under my bikini bottoms and tipping me against his chest.

Exactly where I wanted to be.

Well, almost exactly. I broke the kiss long enough to drag Russell's shirt over his head. Better.

Russell didn't have sculpted muscles like Michael, the muscles I'd lost my mind over almost four years previously. But he ate well and the evidence of his gym sessions showed, which now that I'd taken off my rose-tinted glasses, left him looking just perfect in my eyes.

I deepened the kiss, walking my fingertips up his spine, taking in every contour of his body. The smooth skin. The hint of stubble speckling his jaw. The strong arms and the way I fitted so comfortably into them.

Laughter drifted across as other guests made their way down the path to the beach, and I sent a silent thank you to Emmy not only for engineering this trip in the first place but for the screen of plants and trees that gave the terrace its privacy. Nobody could see us, even if Russell bent me nuddy over the table. Which was a distinct possibility, the way things were going. I mean, I could be naked in seconds. My entire outfit was held together with five bows.

Heat pooled in my belly, and the bulge growing against my stomach? I never would've guessed Russell was packing *that* in his shorts.

I slid a hand between us and copped a feel. Staked my claim. He stiffened in more ways than one.

"Are we moving too quickly?" he asked.

"Right now, we're not moving quick enough."

A pause, and he made up his mind. Fumbled a hand under my hair, and the cover-up pooled at my feet, leaving me in the tiniest bikini Bradley had packed, one I thought I'd never wear until Russell's words last night encouraged me. He tugged the end of the tie.

"I've been wanting to do this since we got here, but I thought you'd castrate me."

"I probably would have at the beginning of the week."

"What changed?"

A good question. Everything, and at the same time, not enough. Not yet. But that didn't stop me from wanting to haul Russell into bed tonight.

"I changed."

That answer seemed to satisfy him, and he cupped my breasts, dipped his head, and drew one nipple into his mouth, sending me halfway to heaven when he sucked. Fire kindled inside of me, igniting, sending sparks through every limb. Sparks that flared into flames when he gave the other breast equal attention.

I tried to undo my bikini bottoms, but he stopped me with a shake of his head.

"Why?" I asked.

"There's no rush." He brought my hand to his lips, kissed each knuckle in turn. "We've got all night, and I want to take my time with you."

He swept my hair to one side and nuzzled my neck, ran the tip of his tongue along my jaw and made goosebumps pop out on my arms. I could practically smell the pheromones mixed in with his woodsy aftershave.

This...this... Was this how it *should* be? Was a man meant to wind you up tighter, tighter, like an elastic band stretching to its snapping point? I was by no means a virgin, but not one man had ever made me feel so vulnerable, so needy, so strung-out with desire. Michael had rubbed away until I came—or pretended to come if I just wanted to get it over with—then taken whatever he wanted. I thought that was normal.

Yet another thing I'd been wrong about, it seemed.

A squeal escaped my lips as Russell picked me up in a move reminiscent of last night, except this time, he didn't part his lips from mine. I clung to him as he kicked the door shut behind him and carried me into my bedroom. Set me on my feet. Lowered me gently onto the bed, still without breaking the kiss.

Somewhere along the way, I'd lost my bikini bottoms, and thank goodness I'd tidied up down there. I'd scoffed when Bradley sent me to get everything waxed "just in case," but now it seemed I owed him a box of chocolates or something.

"Fuck me," Russell muttered when he cupped my mound. "You're bare."

It was the first time I'd heard him curse properly, and the words sent another flash of heat between my legs.

"Say it again."

"You're bare?"

"No, the first part."

"Fuck me?"

"I want to."

I reached for his cock again, but this time, I got a shake of his head plus a smile.

"Not yet."

"But—"

One finger. One finger, that was all it took. One slim finger that trailed through my slick centre then pressed on the sweet spot, sending me arching off the bed. I'd seen those elegant hands dancing over the keyboard a hundred times, but I never realised quite what they were capable of. Or indeed Russell's tongue.

By the time he'd finished with me, I was a quivering mess. Less coherent even than on my first night out of Australia, a night when I'd cried myself to sleep out of anger and fear.

And he was still wearing his bloody shorts.

But this time when I reached for them, he didn't stop me, just raised his hips so I could slide them down to his ankles, and then kicked them off.

"Are you sure about this?" he asked.

"I've been naked underneath you for the past hour. I think if I wasn't, I'd have let you know sooner."

"I like your mouth," he said, leaning in for another kiss before I rolled to the side and yanked open the nightstand drawer. Thank goodness for Akeem and his dirty mind. I selected a condom, tore it open, and rolled it on.

When Russell slid inside, I let out a little giggle at

the squelching noise, but he didn't crack a smile. No, he held my gaze until he was in to the hilt, then closed his eyes on a sigh. Good. It felt so good. Like I'd just found the missing piece of a jigsaw puzzle in the most unexpected place. And when he opened his eyes and started to move, I gave up on any attempt at decorum, screaming and moaning and finally gasping out his name as my third orgasm tore through me. One last thrust, and he came with a soft grunt, returning the favour.

"*Kylie.*"

I buried my face in his neck, trying to blink back the tears gathering, but of course he noticed. When he took his nose out of his computer, he was scarily perceptive.

"What's wrong?" He tried to roll off me, but I tightened my grip. "Are you crying?"

"No. Yes. Sort of. I'm emotional, that's all. Just acting like a girl."

"We all get emotional. Men are just better conditioned to hide it." He kissed the wet tracks on my cheeks. "It's never been like that for me before."

"Me neither."

Now the tears came thick and fast, and this time, Russell did get up. Got up and walked out the door the way I'd done so many times in the past. I'd never returned. Not once. I felt bereft until Russell came back with a clean cotton handkerchief.

"Here." He wiped away the mess, then snuggled me against his chest. Michael had never been a cuddler, and the move left me confused for a moment. I hadn't had anyone to lean on for so, so long, and now the sweetest man was offering me a shoulder to cry on, quite literally. And that only made me more of a wreck.

I'd been the queen of one-night stands for years, but I never wanted this night to end.

CHAPTER 13 - KYLIE

AN UNFAMILIAR RINGING woke me, and it took a moment before I realised it was coming from the phone on the nightstand. The landline, not my mobile. I had no idea where I'd even left that.

"Who's that? What's happened?"

Russell's arm snaked across me, and the events of last night came flooding back. Dinner. Him pulling me across the table. The best sex I'd ever had.

"It's just a wake-up call." He grabbed the receiver, spoke a few words, and hung up again. "I thought that'd be easier than trying to retrieve my phone from the swimming pool in the middle of the night or digging out a spare."

"Oh my gosh. I can't believe I did that. I'm so, so sorry."

"Don't be. It was worth it." He moved back my hair so he could see my eyes. "Are you okay now?"

"Honestly? I have no idea."

And I really didn't, because a thousand thoughts hit me like a freight train. What *was* last night? Hot as hell, obviously, but apart from that? Russell was going home as soon as we either got this mess sorted out or I went to jail, whichever came sooner, and I'd been starting to like him even before he gave me three mind-blowing orgasms. At best, this could be a one-weekend stand, and at the end of it, I'd be left broken no matter what.

No, I wasn't okay.

But rather than try to explain, I just closed my eyes as Russell kissed me on the forehead.

"We can talk later, but Leyton's coming at ten, and I thought you'd want time to freshen up. I left you to sleep as long as I could."

"What time is it?"

"A quarter past nine. And I have a video-conference in fifteen minutes. One of those board meetings I mentioned. Two of my fellow directors are on a working trip to San Francisco and the third still in London's a night owl, hence holding it so early. It shouldn't take more than an hour, but..."

"I understand. You have to work."

"I'd much rather shut out the world and spend the weekend in here with you."

The weekend. Seemed we were on the same page with the timescale. My smile felt shaky, but I hoped it looked sultry, or at the very least, confident.

"We can pick up where we left off later?"

"Too damn right. But as long as Leyton doesn't put me to work again, why don't we go out for a few hours this afternoon first? You can choose the activity this time."

Russell didn't want to go straight back to bed? At first, that disappointed me, but I quickly realised that having a man who wanted me by his side as well as on my back wasn't exactly a bad thing.

"Any preferences?"

"Surprise me."

Surprise him. No golf, no sharks, no alcohol. What

did that leave?

"You seem edgy this morning," Leyton said when I sat down with him on the terrace. Russell had commandeered the living room for his conference call.

"Edgy? How?"

"Sort of...smiley but nervous?"

That just about summed up the current state of affairs. "I guess I'm just worried about tomorrow. How's it going?"

"We've had some difficult questions from the Feds regarding where our information's coming from and why we're getting it, but we've sidestepped them so far."

"So far?"

"That's why I'm here to talk to you. We want to put a backup plan in place in case you have to leave in a hurry. If anyone works out you're our source, this place is connected to Blackwood."

My guts clenched. "You think something's gonna go wrong?"

"There's no reason why it should. Call it Mimi and her paranoia, but she's insisting. We've got a pilot on standby to get you out of here if the need arises, but do you have a preference over where you'd want to go?"

This wasn't so much an emotional rollercoaster as an emotional stunt plane. The constant loop-the-loops and sharp turns left my insides churning. But deep down, I'd known this might happen, and at least I was getting some help with my escape. I should pack a bag, get ready.

"Morocco's next on my list."

"Morocco. Okay, we can do that." Leyton drained the last of his coffee and stood. "I should get back and make the arrangements."

"That's it? Don't you need to talk to Russell?"

"No, I just wanted to speak to you in person about this." Leyton's mask of professionalism slipped for a second. "Fuck, we all know Brenner and Mills are guilty, but they're slippery as hell. What you're going through...this never should've happened."

"But it did."

"I promise I'm doing everything I can. Everyone at Blackwood is."

Yes, they were, and I was more grateful for that than they'd ever know. But would it be enough?

"Did you make a decision?" Russell asked.

With the villa to ourselves again, he pulled me in for a kiss, and the moment our tongues touched, I sank into his arms. He stole my breath, his heart beating against mine. I was lost, but at the same time, I was found.

Back when we were teenagers, Chloe used to tell me it was always the quiet ones, and I never understood quite what she meant. But now I did.

"Yes, I made a decision." *Inhale, Kylie. Exhale.* "Jet skiing. We're going jet skiing."

Russell went rigid. "Isn't that dangerous?"

"Not really. Sharks don't often jump out of the water."

"Define 'not often.'"

"Maybe once or twice. Just don't look on YouTube."

"You're not exactly filling me with confidence."

"Trust me, it'll be okay." I tried to push him towards the bedroom to change, but he stopped me. Held me still then cupped my face in his hands.

"I trust you, Kylie."

He held my gaze, and that was it. I broke. Completely broke. For so long, I'd tried to stay strong, but every time an obstacle got thrown in my path, the scramble over or around or through it sapped a little more of my energy. And Russell had spent the past few days knocking the last of my walls down, whether he realised it or not. Nobody had *ever* said those words to me. Not my parents, not Chloe, and certainly not Michael. To me, they were worth a million of the glib "I love yous" he'd tossed in my direction.

Russell bundled me up and held me close, kissing my forehead, my hair, my temples.

"Sorry, darling. I didn't mean to make you cry."

"You didn't."

"So this is just one hell of a coincidence?"

"I don't... It's just..."

"Shh. I've got you. I'll always have you, if you'll let me."

"What do you mean? I thought this was just a fling?"

"I hate to break it to you, Kylie, but I don't do flings."

He was joking, surely? "But...but where can we possibly go with this?"

"I'll admit things look bleak at the moment, but I'm not giving up, and neither should you. The more time I spend with you, the more time I want to spend with you. And today, it looks like that time'll be spent jet skiing."

I buried my head against his chest and squeezed him as tight as I could, both overwhelmed and terrified at the same time. I never wanted to let him go. What did he see in me? I had no idea, but the feeling of desire was mutual. The more I got of him, the more I wanted. A tiny glimmer of hope flickered inside me, a spark, but darkness quickly descended again. Because what hope did we have?

"Okay."

"Okay." He raised my chin and kissed me softly—almost chastely—on the lips. "What does one need for jet skiing?"

Oh, hell, he was so bloody posh. "Just yourself. And some sunblock."

"Are you driving?"

"Unless you want to? Or we could take separate jet skis?"

"No, I like the idea of you being nestled between my legs all afternoon." He blew out a breath. "It might kill me, but I like the idea."

Until then, I'd been focusing on the wildlife-spotting aspect of the trip, not Russell's freaking trouser snake. But the prospect of having him wrapped around me for an hour or two was undeniably attractive, even if it made me self-combust.

"I'll drive."

The water lapped at the edges of the jet ski as we rested in a small cove a little way up the coast. The ride had been every bit as good and bad as I'd imagined. We'd cut through channels and ridden around small islands, taking in only a fraction of the breathtaking scenery Queensland had to offer. Russell even spotted a dolphin in the distance, leaping out of the water in a show just for us.

But my insides were on fire, and Russell kissing my neck didn't help one bit.

"That was wild," he murmured. "Perhaps even better than golf." His hands crept under my T-shirt and cupped my breasts, thumbs circling my nipples until they hardened into stiff peaks. "Definitely better than golf."

"You're such a perv."

Teeth nibbled at my earlobe. "Would you rather I stopped?"

I quickly shook my head, arching back into him, pressing into his hands. The movement elicited a low groan, and I reached behind me to see what other effect it might be having. Russell was half hard already.

"We should head back," I whispered, my voice soft because, in truth, I was happy exactly where I was. "Don't you think?"

"No, I think we should make out on a jet ski. That's got to come under advanced skills, right?"

I twisted to look at him. Ran my tongue over his bottom lip and then sucked it. My head reminded me I should have been packing, getting ready for whatever tomorrow threw at me, but my body had other ideas, and I tangled my fingers in Russell's hair, pulling him into me until my back protested. I wanted him. Craved him. When my muscles threatened to spasm, I loosened my grip and swung my leg over the seat so I was facing him properly, his cock pressing between my legs. Another groan.

Small waves pushed at the jet ski, rocking me into him, and when I leaned forward slightly, he rubbed me in exactly the right spot. I tore his shirt off, then mine, relishing the feel of skin on skin, our bodies slick with sweat that had nothing to do with the sun. I pulled back for a moment to glance around. No, we were completely alone, with nothing but the noise of the birds for company.

Russell seemed to share my thoughts because he popped one breast out of my bikini top, leaning down to run his tongue over my nipple. I let out a squeak, half surprise, half pleasure. Michael had been dangerous, but at that moment, I realised Russell was too. This man would steal my heart if I let him.

I tried to even things up, reaching down to push his swim shorts lower on his hips. His cock sprang free, and I gripped it. Ran a thumb across the tip, swirling the drop of pre-cum over the end, then rubbed the hardness against myself. Only a tiny piece of material stood between us, and it was so, so tempting to push it aside, to slide myself forward until I had Russell exactly where I wanted him. But I'd stopped taking the pill years ago. Egypt wasn't exactly famed for its easy access to birth control.

But then I saw Russell was holding a tiny packet in his hand.

"Do it," he said.

"You brought a condom?"

He shrugged. "I thought we might find a quiet beach somewhere. Hoped we would. But this'll do, and I don't think I can last much longer."

I snatched the packet from him and tore into it with my teeth. A moment later, I inched forward, slowly, slowly, until he got sick of waiting and met me with a buck of his hips. Oh, fuck. I buried my face against his chest to keep from crying out as he thrust in and out of me, then bit his shoulder when I shattered around him.

"Sorry," I whispered.

"Don't be."

He came with a quiet groan seconds later and collapsed against me, the two of us wrapped up tight in each other's arms.

Shit, shit, shit. I was gone for this man.

CHAPTER 14 - KYLIE

IN MANY WAYS, the waiting was the hardest part. Late on Sunday evening, I paced the living room, hungry but unable to eat. Leyton had called half an hour ago to say everything was in place. Russell had his three laptops set up, alerts ready and waiting to deliver news of any police activity in the Brisbane area, but so far, nothing seemed to be happening.

"What do you think of this house?" Russell asked.

"What house?"

I sat on his lap, forcing myself to stop fretting for a moment and focus on the centre screen. Russell was looking at interior shots from a three-bedroom villa in Marrakech.

"Why are you looking at a house in Morocco?"

"Just planning for every eventuality."

"Are you crazy?"

"Yes. About you."

"You can't seriously be considering renting a house in Marrakech?"

"I'm not. I'm considering buying a house in Marrakech. That way, we could pick our own decor."

A tear leaked out and plopped onto his keyboard. Russell wiped the ones that followed away with his thumbs, then followed up with a kiss to each cheek.

"You can't move to Morocco," I told him.

"Which part of 'I don't do flings' didn't you understand?"

"I didn't think you were serious. I mean, why do you even like me? You could have any girl you wanted."

"Yes, and now that I've got her, I'm keeping her."

"Why? Why me? Two months ago, you were into Tai."

In Egypt, they'd gone out for dinner together, several times in fact. It only ended when she fell for our neighbour in a bizarre case of opposites attract.

"For the most part, that was a pretence. We had a deal. Tai posed as my girlfriend to keep my brother from lecturing me about work/life balance, and I bought her dinner. Every time Finn caught me working, he tried to set me up with another vapid idiot, so the arrangement worked quite well."

"For the most part?" Why was I even upset? Tai was besotted with Ren, for crying out loud. Yesterday, she'd messaged to tell me they were picking out new furniture for his house. "So there *was* something there?"

"Don't do this, Kylie."

"But I don't understand why you want *me*. There's a warrant out for my freaking arrest!"

"For something you didn't do."

"You think that matters? The police don't care."

I tried to get up but Russell held me down, hugging me tightly. "From the very first moment we met, it was always you. Even when you pushed me to date Tai. I thought you weren't interested, and yes, Tai was sweet. I'll admit it's possible our relationship would have gone beyond a business arrangement if everything else hadn't happened." He gave me a lopsided smile.

"Maybe I'd have reconsidered my position on flings. But the events in Egypt *did* happen, and now I've got you exactly where I want you."

"But why me?"

"First, there's the obvious. You're beautiful, and I won't deny that's why you caught my eye. But you're also brave, and smart, and loyal. And living here with you this week's shown me how easy you are to get along with. You don't nag when I get engrossed in work, you're not high maintenance, and you're adventurous." He gave his head a little shake. "Jet ski sex. Didn't see that one coming."

"Not high maintenance? You're talking about moving to bloody Morocco to be with me!"

"Yes, and I bet when I get there, you won't berate me for wearing the wrong colour tie to the opera or forgetting to order more caviar from Fortnum & Mason."

The exasperation in his voice suggested he spoke from experience.

"Someone really did that?"

"Yes, someone really did. Which is why she's an ex-girlfriend and you're very much not."

"Oh."

"Yes, oh. And don't even consider pushing me away, because I'm not going anywhere." He turned back to the screen. "So, the backup plan—do you like this place? Or should I look at somewhere else?"

"I'd live in a shack with you."

The corners of his lips twitched. "Sorry, darling, but I don't do shacks either."

A *ping* sounded, and a box popped up in the corner of the screen. In an instant, Russell went from playful to serious, reaching around me to punch keys and click stuff.

"Looks like something's happening," he said.

"What? What's happening? Is it Nabarra Street?"

"No, it's not... Shots fired at Delario's Pizzeria. It could be nothing to do with us."

But it was. How glad I was that I hadn't eaten because my stomach clenched and heaved. It was everything to do with us.

"Kylie, what's wrong?"

"Who got hurt? Does it say?"

"It doesn't say anyone got hurt. It's just a post on Twitter. Why?"

"Shane's mum owns that restaurant."

Since Michael was as bad at cooking as me, it'd been our go-to place for dinner after an evening shift. The dough was always soggy, but on the rare occasions I suggested going somewhere else for pizza, Michael had reminded me that cop families stuck together. Mrs. Chapman offered a twenty percent discount to anyone with a warrant card. Half of the force went there for takeout. What the hell was going on? Had one of my former colleagues been injured? Or worse?

All we could do was watch as the story unravelled, tweet by tweet, news headline by news headline, interview by solemn interview.

A little after 10 p.m., the Australian Federal Police had raided Delario's Pizzeria and found a large quantity of drugs. While trying to arrest the people involved, guns had been drawn, resulting in the death of one officer and the injury of another.

"Who's been shot?" I asked, back to pacing again. *Please, let it be Michael.*

Not that I wanted him dead—I wouldn't have wished that on anyone—but when it came down to his life or somebody else's, I knew who I'd rather stopped breathing.

"They're not saying yet. Someone on Twitter reckons a guy from the Specialist Response Group was down. Isn't that like the Australian version of a SWAT team?"

I bit back a stream of curses. "Yes, it is."

Had my actions resulted in his death?

"Hold on, there's something about Nabarra Street here. The occupants of a house there have been arrested."

"Did anyone get hurt?"

"It doesn't look that way."

Thank goodness.

It wasn't until after midnight that we found out all the horrible, devastating details. Leyton arrived with Mimi trailing along behind him like a tiny, pissed-off wraith.

"What happened?" I asked. I was shaking by then, trembling from head to toe due to stress, fear, and lack of food. I hadn't eaten a thing since breakfast. Couldn't.

"The AFP cornered Michael and Owen, and they panicked. Started shooting. One of the SRG team took a round to the chest, and Owen's in the operating theatre as we speak."

"Will Owen be okay? I mean, will he live?"

"That's all the information I have on him right now."

"What about Michael?"

A look passed between Leyton and Mimi, and I knew the news wasn't good.

"He got away," she said. "In the middle of the chaos, he stole a car and ran."

"What?" My words sounded hollow, even to my own ears. That was a scenario I hadn't really considered. Michael was on the run? The thought terrified me in case he hurt somebody else, but a small part of me thought *see how you like it, asshole*. "Who shot the cop? The news said he was dead?"

"Died on the way to the hospital," Leyton said. "The ballistics haven't come back yet. Too soon."

"Oh, hell." I collapsed onto the sofa, numb. "This is all my fault."

"No," Mimi said. "It's Michael and Owen's fault. Nobody asked them to load enough coke, heroin, and ecstasy for every junkie in Queensland into the back of an unmarked police car and drive it through the city."

"Are you kidding?" I turned to Leyton. "Is she kidding?"

"Nope. The coke and heroine were packed into flour bags, and the ecstasy was disguised as kids' candy."

"Holy fuck."

What if a child had gotten hold of it? That didn't bear thinking about.

"Holy fuck indeed. So far, they've arrested Owen Mills, Charlene Chapman, a chef, two waiters, and three delivery drivers, plus two women back at Nabarra Street who claim they've never heard of Francis Mulhearn."

"Shane's mother? They arrested Shane's *mother*?"

Mimi shrugged. "She was the one who started shooting first."

I struggled to believe it. To me, Mrs. Chapman was a sweet middle-aged lady who always put too much tomato sauce on pizza and gave me twice as many slightly dried-out dough balls as I'd ordered. I couldn't even imagine her holding a gun, let alone firing one. I'd been the most awful judge of character back then, hadn't I? But what about now? I thought Russell was the one, but what if underneath that kind veneer he was actually a slimeball, just waiting to ooze out?

No. *No*, I couldn't think like that. Russell was no Michael.

"Mulhearn got away?" Russell asked.

"Unfortunately. When they went into the house, he'd vanished."

Two men in the wind, undoubtedly with money and connections. The news just got worse and worse.

"Is that Brenner's laptop?" Russell asked, nodding at the slim black bag slung over Mimi's shoulder.

She nodded once. "Yes."

"Do you reckon he'll come back looking for it?"

"We've left two colleagues behind at the house just in case, but I don't think so. He didn't have a go-bag waiting, and if I was in his shoes, I wouldn't show my face back home."

Russell held out a hand for the bag. "Then I'd better get started."

After Leyton and Mimi left, Russell got his head down behind Michael's laptop for the rest of the evening and part of the night. I brought him coffee, made sure he ate, and we had fifteen minutes of light relief where I attempted to teach him yoga on the terrace. Aurelie had left the mats behind after our session on Tuesday, so I figured we might as well make use of them.

He crawled into bed in the early hours, spooning himself tightly against me, his front to my back, one arm curled around my waist. I hadn't slept a wink until that point, but with him there, I felt safe. Secure enough to close my eyes and snooze, albeit restlessly.

When my eyes flickered open, sunlight was slanting through a gap in the curtains, and a hard cock pressed against my ass. What a way to wake up. Russell was still breathing steadily, but when I nestled back against him, he murmured something unintelligible.

"Are you awake?" I whispered.

"Barely. What time is it?"

I checked my phone on the nightstand. "Eight o'clock."

"Rats. I should get up."

I wiggled a little more. "You're already up. Spare me five minutes before you get out of bed?"

Russell smoothed my tangle of hair out of the way, giving himself better access to my neck. His lips were so soft, so gentle. Not sloppy, not pushy, just sweet. I treasured every one of his kisses.

"No, but I can spare you fifteen."

For the first time in my life, I got to experience sleepy morning sex, and it might even have been my new favourite thing. When Russell slid a hand between my legs to finish me off, I had to bite the pillow to stop from crying out. Thoughts jumbled around in my head. *More, more, more... I'm in trouble... Harder... I could so easily love this man if I let myself.*

The mess just kept getting messier.

I turned on the TV that morning, hating every moment of every show, but still feeling compelled to keep watching. One channel showed a picture of last night's haul—ten kilos of coke, five of heroin, and eight thousand ecstasy pills. The street value ran into millions. No wonder Froggy had been so paranoid and Michael so secretive.

By afternoon, the news anchors began reporting more about the situation. Apparently, Michael and company had used Delario's Pizzeria as a base of operations, and the food deliveries had been a cover for distributing drugs. Pizza and coke? No problem.

How had I been so stupid? So blind to what was going on under my own nose? My ex-boyfriend had run possibly the largest drugs ring in Queensland's history.

By early evening, some enterprising researcher put two and two together and linked us. I knew it would happen, but it still made me sick to see my picture up there alongside Michael's, and when they began speculating that we were partners in crime and on the run together, fury took over.

How dare they think I had anything to do with selling drugs? There was no evidence of that at all. None!

"I don't believe this!" I muttered, making coffee to occupy my hands. Otherwise, I might have been tempted to punch something.

Russell glanced up from his spot at the table. "That you're a hardened criminal? Neither do I, so that's something else we've got in common."

"How's it going with the laptop? Did you find anything yet?"

"Some of Mulhearn's paranoia seems to have rubbed off on Brenner. He's got passwords on everything, and half of the stuff's encrypted."

"Can you get through it?"

"Most probably, but not as quickly as we'd both like. Blackwood's tech team's working on it too."

"Is there any clue as to where he went?"

"Not yet."

Yes, waiting was definitely the hardest part.

CHAPTER 15 - KYLIE

LEYTON SHOWED UP early on Tuesday morning. Thankfully not too early. Fifteen minutes sooner, and Russell and I would've been otherwise engaged. Leyton took one look at me—my flushed face and guilty expression—and raised an eyebrow.

"Did I interrupt something?"

"Uh, I was just doing yoga. You know, to relax?" Russell and I hadn't discussed telling anyone about the change in our relationship yet, and I didn't want to jump the gun by suggesting we were more than just friends. "It's hot out there. Do you have any news?"

"Maybe."

I moved aside so Leyton could come in, then closed the door behind him. Russell was already working, and thankfully looking far more composed than me.

"What's up?" he asked.

"I'm on my way to Sunshine Coast Airport. A man fitting Francis Mulhearn's description rented a plane and took off from there yesterday evening with a passenger."

"You think it was Mulhearn and Brenner?"

"The Feds do. The pair filed a flight plan for Indonesia, and Mimi's packing already."

"She's going after them?" I asked.

"Mimi doesn't like the bad guys to win. None of us

do. Kind of ironic, though, don't you think? That they're the ones running now?"

"I'd had that thought."

"I found some stuff on Indonesia in Brenner's search history," Russell said. "Plus Vietnam, Malaysia, and Thailand."

"What sort of stuff?" Leyton asked. "Information that could help a criminal on the run?"

"It looked more like vacation planning. Hotels, excursions, and, uh, tourist attractions."

"What kind of tourist attractions?"

Russell frowned slightly. "I'm not sure that's important right now."

What didn't he want me to know? "I appreciate that you're trying to protect me, but there's no need. I'm not a porcelain doll."

Russell let out a long sigh. "Fine. It was brothels. He was researching brothels."

Stay calm, Kylie. Okay, Russell was right. Again. I really didn't want to know that.

Leyton just nodded, as if the fact that my ex paid for sex was a perfectly normal, everyday occurrence. "Can you summarise the information? I'll pass it on to the team."

Russell murmured his agreement, and I forced myself to focus on my breathing. *In and out. In and out. In and out.* For once, I was glad Mimi was a psycho, because I couldn't think of a better person to pay Michael a surprise visit.

"Do you want a coffee or anything before you go?" I asked Leyton. "A pastry? Akeem sent a whole basketful over this morning."

"Nah, I ate in the office. I'll keep you updated,

okay?"

I thought it would be another lonely morning, just me and the TV, but two minutes after Leyton left, there was a soft knock at the door. Not Akeem—he always hammered on the wood or wandered around to the terrace if we didn't let him in fast enough.

I opened the door and found Aurelie standing there.

"Hi. Akeem sent me over to give you a yoga lesson. Or meditation, whatever you want. He thought you could use some company."

What on earth was Akeem thinking?

"That's kind of you—of him—but I'm quite busy today."

"Are you sure? I could come back later if—"

"Totally sure. But thanks anyway."

I closed the door then leaned on it, feeling guilty and nervous at the same time. Aurelie seemed lovely but also overly curious. I hated the way she studied me.

"Everything okay?" Russell asked.

"Fine."

Yoga wasn't actually a bad idea. A few asanas could help to calm my nerves as long as I did them alone rather than under the watchful eyes of an all-too-perceptive yoga teacher. While Russell turned back to Michael's laptop, I headed out to the mats on the terrace, one blue and one green, waiting under the dappled shade of a jacaranda tree.

While I was away, I'd learned to take pleasure in the small things, those little gifts that everyone else took for granted. The rays of the sun. Breathing fresh air. Cool tiles under bare feet, the smell of fresh coffee, the sound of the birds in the trees, the feel of the breeze on my face.

For the last three years, my motto had been to live each day as if it was my last, and I took that to heart as I stretched out my calves and settled into downwards-facing dog.

Perhaps today *would* be my last?

An hour and a half later, my muscles burned, and when I tried to lift into wheel pose, my arms wobbled and gave way. I fell onto my ass. Yup, it was time for a shower.

Russell grabbed my hand as I walked past, brought it to his lips, and kissed my palm. Such a simple gesture, but I loved it. I loved *him*.

Oh, shit.

I *loved* him.

CHAPTER 16 - KYLIE

"I'M ALL SWEATY," I choked out as the enormity of the revelation struck me like a wrecking ball. Not the revelation that I was sweaty. The revelation that I was in *love* with Russell. This was big.

"I don't care about a little sweat," he said, completely unaware that I was freaking out inside.

"Maybe I'll take a shower anyway."

I needed to *think*.

"Whatever you want." His lips tickled as he curled my hand closed and brushed them across my knuckles. "I'm not going anywhere."

Russell went back to work, focused as always, while I stumbled into the bathroom, desperately trying to process my thoughts. He cared. Even when work took precedence and he was in the middle of an important task, there was a part of him that cared. I'd finally found him. My soulmate. The man who stole my breath, my heart, and sometimes my sanity. Some said finding the perfect man was the difficult part, but I knew that was a lie. Keeping him would be a thousand times harder.

In the bathroom, I let the hot water cascade over me, hoping it would wash away the filth that clung under my skin. That was just wishful thinking. The muck had been ingrained for years, and getting rid of it would take more than fancy toiletries.

What should I do? The noble thing would be to let Russell go, to vanish quietly into the night instead of dragging him into whatever pit I ended up in. He had a life in London. A job. Friends.

I had nothing.

And yet, I couldn't quite bring myself to sever the connection.

When my skin began going wrinkly, I shut off the water and shrugged into the fluffy white bathrobe hanging on the back of the door. My stomach told me it was lunchtime, and I needed to make sure Russell ate. Perhaps I could call Akeem and ask—

"Heard you were back in town."

The first word sent tremors down my spine. The second made my heart drop to my feet. The rest? They tore the bottom out of my world. That pit I mentioned? I'd just fallen through the bottom of it and straight into hell.

"W-w-what are you doing here?"

Michael sat on the edge of the bed, seemingly relaxed, legs spread in the cocky way that only men could manage, a semi-automatic resting in his lap. Where the hell was Russell? I looked past Michael, through to the lounge, and saw a body sprawled on the floor beyond the dining table. Fuck! Russell wasn't moving.

I edged towards the door, but Michael motioned me back with the gun.

"I'm here to catch up. You and me, we've got a lot to talk about." He stood, and his stance turned menacing. "Like what the fuck you think you're playing at."

He spat the words at me, and a drop of saliva

landed on my cheek. I didn't dare to wipe it away.

"What *I'm* playing at?" A flicker of yesterday's anger stirred inside me, but I did my best to temper it. No point in stoking Michael's wrath even further. "You framed me for murder!"

"Not really. You practically framed yourself when you agreed to meet Jasper John. How many times did I have to tell you? *If you get a tip, tell me first.* Such a simple rule, and you broke it."

"I was doing my job."

"Your job was to obey orders."

"So you could bury the evidence?"

"So I could encourage an appropriate narrative."

"You mean threaten people."

"I prefer the term incentivise."

"Why are we even having this conversation?" I needed to get to Russell. He hadn't moved, not even a twitch. Was he dead? Had Michael killed him? Tears threatened to burst out of me along with my rising fury. "What the hell do you want from me?"

"You've ruined my fucking life, Kylie Jaye, and you need to fix what you've done."

"You were the one dealing drugs!"

"Supply and demand. If it wasn't me, it would've been someone else. And you sure enjoyed the fruits of my labours while we were together. The diamond earrings I gave you for your birthday? The trip to Bali? Tickets to see your favourite rock bands? Where do you think all the money came from?"

"I didn't know! I didn't think—"

"Exactly. You didn't think. You never thought, Kylie. That was one of the things I liked about you."

Instinct took over and I moved to slap him, but he

caught my hand and forced me back against the wall.

"Didn't you ever wonder why I picked you for Task Force Titan? It wasn't for your brains. It was for these." He reached out and squeezed a breast. Hard. If he hadn't been holding a gun, I'd have broken his damn fingers. "Made us look good for the diversity committee."

"You're sick."

"Aw, babe, you used to like that."

"What do you want from me?" I asked again.

"Simple. You're going to walk into the police station and tell everyone the drugs were your idea. That you..." His lips curved into a thin smile. "Corrupted me."

"Nobody's gonna believe that. Are you crazy?"

"The story doesn't need to stand up to scrutiny. I just need long enough to get out of the country. And I see your boyfriend has my laptop, so I suppose I should thank him for that. Saves me from getting a new one."

"Why didn't you just leave with Francis Mulhearn?"

"Who?"

"Froggy."

"Francis? That's his real name? Well, little girl, *Francis* wants to kill me because he reckons it's my fault that seven million dollars' worth of his drugs got seized. But there's no way I spilled the beans. The leak must've been from his end."

That was Michael all over—arrogant and rude. Nothing was ever his fault.

But I nodded and agreed because it was better for him to think that Mulhearn was at fault than to work out we had his Ether messages.

"He should've been more careful, shouldn't he?"

Michael's smile turned triumphant. I risked a quick

glance in Russell's direction, but he still hadn't moved. I couldn't see any blood, and I hadn't heard a gunshot. That had to be a good sign, right? Inside, I was cracking. I felt as though the slightest touch would shatter me, but I couldn't fall apart. Not now, not when there was a chance of saving Russell.

"We *all* should've been more careful," I continued. "How did you find me, anyway?"

Where had it all gone wrong? Would he tell me? Of course he'd tell me—Michael was a natural-born show-off.

"When you got away from Shane on the bike, I knew you had help, and there's only one crew in Brisbane with enough balls to pull a stunt like that. Then I saw Leyton Rix outside the morgue on Wednesday morning, and it all clicked into place. I've been tracking his phone ever since, and he kept coming here. I don't know how you managed to afford Blackwood's services, but..." Michael looked around, nodding slowly. "I must say, you've done well for yourself, Kylie. I thought you'd end up on the streets somewhere, spreading your legs for money, but I guess you found yourself a sucker who'd pay a better price."

"I hate you."

Michael just laughed. "Hate that you're not as smart as me, more like." He glanced at his watch and motioned towards the door. "Let's go."

"To the police station? Why the hell should I? You've already taken everything from me; why should I give you what you want?"

"Simple. You've got two parents happily enjoying their retirement, and I'm sure you want them to carry on that way."

"You're threatening my parents now?"

"As I said—consider it an incentive to do the right thing. And don't think for a second that I'm going to let you go running off to Blackwood so they can put your parents into protective custody—I have an associate with them right now, and while you make your confession to the cops, me and your mum and dad will take a little trip. Once I'm happy you're cooperating, I'll let them go."

"And then what? You'll just disappear?"

"Now you're beginning to understand. Get dressed."

"But—"

"Get. Dressed." Michael grabbed my bathrobe and yanked it open, pausing to take a good look. "Still as hot as ever, babe. If only we had more time."

That sick... Wait. Where was Russell? His spot on the floor was empty, and I couldn't see any sign of him. *Please, say he'd gone for help.* How long would the police take to get to the Black Diamond Resort? The nearest police station was in—

"Kylie, get your ass in gear. Stop stalling and put on something nice for your mug shot. The whole world's gonna see that picture."

He grabbed the robe again, and the next part happened in slow motion. A blurred form rushed through the doorway, heading for Michael, arms outstretched.

"Don't touch her!"

I wanted to tell Russell to stop, to run, to get the hell out of there, but all that came out was a scream as Michael raised his gun and fired. A scarlet stain blossomed on Russell's T-shirt, and he gasped for breath as he staggered back into the living room and crumpled to the floor.

His blood wasn't the only red I saw. Rage clouded my vision, and I grabbed the first thing to hand. The model of Shadow, two kilos of solid bronze. I swung it at Michael with every bit of strength I had left, and an expression of surprise froze on his face as I caught him under the chin. Even when he fell, I didn't stop hitting him until I heard another scream. Not mine—this one came from the lounge.

My vision cleared, and I saw Michael lying in front of me, his face caved in, his head misshapen. Aurelie stood in the doorway with her mouth open, staring at my blood-streaked hand.

"Oh my gosh," she whispered.

"I...I..." I couldn't explain. I didn't even know where to start with explaining. "I..."

"Is that him? Your ex?"

What? How did she know? "Yes. Please, help Russell. I don't care about anything else, just help him."

I tried to move, but my limbs were stiff, uncooperative, my brain still trying to process what was happening. What I'd just done. Was Michael dead? Where was the gun? *Get the gun, get the gun, get the gun.*

I spotted the pistol and dropped the magazine out, then kicked it under the bed out of reach in case Michael somehow managed to move. In the living room, Aurelie refocused and dropped to her knees beside Russell.

"He's bleeding."

"Michael shot him." My voice sounded weird, echoey, as if it was coming from somebody else. I jammed two fingers against the bastard's carotid artery, feeling for a pulse.

"What do I do?" Aurelie asked. "Does he need CPR?"

"Is he breathing?" Let Russell be alive. *Please, let him be alive.* I'd give my freedom, my soul, every breath I had left if it meant he'd live.

"I don't..." Aurelie bent forwards, holding the back of her hand by Russell's nose. "Yes, I think so." She fumbled for her phone. "I need to call Akeem."

Nothing from Michael, not even a flutter. Good.

"Akeem? We need an ambulance, not freaking Akeem?"

But she didn't listen, just dialled. Dammit, where was my phone? I spotted it on the floor, smashed, and cursed Michael all over again.

"Akeem? Russell just got shot in Emmy's villa. Is Glenn home? ... Oh, thank goodness." A pause. "Uh, in his chest. I don't know, he's lying on his back. Yes. Okay." She pulled up his shirt, and there was the wound, less than a centimetre across, but oh-so-deadly. "He says to seal the hole." Aurelie grabbed my hand as I crouched beside her and positioned it flat against Russell's ribs. "Press here."

"Who's Glenn? Who are you speaking to?"

"Akeem's boyfriend. He's a doctor, and he's on his way."

"On his way from where? We still need an ambulance!"

"From the staff block. Akeem's calling the ambulance. Do you need to leave?"

"Leave? I can't leave."

"But I thought you were, like, a fugitive?"

"Who told you that?"

"I recognised you from the TV. But when I called Emmy to ask if it was okay, you staying here and everything, she said the stories about you were all rubbish and you didn't do any of the stuff they said you did. She told me to look out for you and be a friend if you needed one, but I was too late. Oh, dammit, I was too late."

Aurelie was on my side? I was literally the worst judge of character in the history of the world. And now Russell was dying because of my past mistakes. *Mine.* As if he knew what I was thinking, he let out a groan that made every hair stand up. Was this the end?

"It's okay. I'm here, and I'm not going anywhere. I promise."

Blood seeped from underneath him now, spreading across the floor and soaking into my gaping bathrobe. Damn Michael. Damn him to hell! If I could've gone back and killed him again, I would have.

The *slap, slap, slap* of running feet sounded on the tile outside, and a black man I'd never seen before skidded into the bedroom, carrying a green bag with a white cross on the side. Was this Glenn?

"Is that the wound under your hand? Keep the pressure on while I check his vitals, okay?"

Thank goodness. Somebody who knew more about first aid than me was there, which meant Russell at least stood a chance.

"He got shot."

"Just the once?"

How could he stay so calm? "Yes, just once."

"We've got a pulse. Not as strong as I'd like, but it's there. Just keep pressing, sweetheart, that's it. I'm going to check a few more things."

It was as if it wasn't really me in that room, watching my worst nightmares come true. The man I loved, lying on the floor, barely breathing. The hiss as Glenn stuck a huge needle between Russell's ribs and let the air escape from his chest cavity. The blood, so much blood. I squeezed Russell's hand, telling him I loved him, telling him I was still there and I'd never leave him. Could he hear me? Could he hear my lie?

"You really need to go," Aurelie said. "There's a dead body in the bedroom, and the police are gonna come."

I shook my head.

"You can take my car. It's parked by the staff block. Or a jet ski?"

"I can't."

"What about a boat? I could call someone to help."

At the mention of help, another disjointed memory surfaced and my heart stuttered. "Michael said he had somebody watching my parents." I felt faint, fuzzy, but when I tried to suck in air, I couldn't breathe. "I need to get to them, but...but..."

"I'll call Blackwood, I promise. They'll know what to do. But please, please leave now."

"I can't."

If one more minute with Russell was all I had left, then I'd take it, no matter how bad the consequences would be. Tears rolled down my cheeks and splashed onto the tiles, and as I shivered, Aurelie wrapped an arm around me, offering support as she murmured quietly into the phone. Her kindness only made me cry harder.

"Please be okay," I whispered to Russell.

The ambulance arrived, and with it came a horde of

my former colleagues. I even recognised a couple of them. When the EMTs lifted Russell onto a stretcher, more blood dripped onto the floor, and my knees buckled. Akeem caught me.

"Sorry, sorry, sorry. We tried to stop the cops from coming, but the moment they heard the word 'gunshot'..."

"Don't worry, I understand."

"It'll be okay," he muttered.

How? How would it be okay?

"Kylie Nichols?" one of the cops said. "I'm arresting you for the murder of Jasper John and..." He glanced across at Michael, but there wasn't much left that was recognisable. "And, uh, someone else."

I tried to follow after Russell, but the cop pulled me back. The click of him handcuffing me barely registered. All I could think about was Russell and how I'd destroyed not only my own life but his as well. The room, the people, the endless voices—they all blurred as I let myself fall into the abyss.

CHAPTER 17 - RUSS

WHAT THE HECK happened? Russell Weisz felt as though he'd been hit in the chest by a bus. A double-decker, no less. Had he? So many ugly scenes had run through his mind over the past... How long had it been? It felt like years.

Bright red buses on a London street, splashing through puddles of blood after another terrorist attack. So real, so vivid. A fight with his brother in a tiny window-less bathroom set amidst bodies piled high in the desert. And worst—by far the worst—a madman shooting him and then doing the same to Kylie.

Kylie. Where was Kylie? He tried to open his eyes, but they didn't want to cooperate. Every breath was a struggle, a desperate attempt to suck in air despite the agony. And what was that bloody beeping?

Russell listened, trying to work out where he was. Not at the resort, he was certain of that. The villa smelled of frangipani and coffee and that vanilla stuff Kylie used in the shower, but this place had a hint of the medicinal about it.

He tried again with the eyes. Got one open. White. Everything was white except for the blurry figure sitting on the other side of the room with a laptop. Was that him? Was this some sort of strange out-of-body experience?

"Welcome back, mate."

Russell recognised that voice, but where from? Not Australia. Not London, although the accent was British. Virginia? Yes, he'd heard it in Virginia.

"Luke?" he tried to say, but it came out as a croak. "Luke?" Better.

Luke was one of Emmy Black's tech gurus. Russell had met him at Riverley, and they'd had a few lively discussions over beers when everyone else had gone to bed. Luke knew his stuff, and if there was anyone from the US that Russell was glad to see, it was him.

"Don't try to move. I'll get the nurse."

"Nurse? What..." A cough. His mouth was drier than the Sahara. "What happened?"

"You got shot."

Shot? *Shot?* Oh, fuck. It hadn't been a dream. It was true!

"Kylie... Where's Kylie?"

Russell tried to get out of bed, but Luke shoved the laptop to one side and gently pushed him back down. "Easy, buddy. Stay still. Kylie's...she's okay."

"Where is she? Is she hurt?"

Geez, every inhale felt like breathing in fire.

"She's safe. Stay still, okay? I'll get the nurse."

"Why are *you* here?"

"Apparently, I'm on vacation."

Fifteen minutes later, Russell had been poked and prodded, had his vital signs checked, and gotten a stern lecture from the doctor on the risks of playing hero. But none of them would answer his questions. Where was his girlfriend? And the bastard who shot him?

Finally, the medical team trooped out, and ten seconds later, a shadow slipped into the room, wraith-like. Mimi Tran. Russell let out a groan, because wasn't this day bad enough already? Kylie wasn't fond of the woman, and quite frankly, she made Russell very nervous.

But maybe he'd finally get some answers now?

"Where's Kylie?" he asked for what seemed like the hundredth time.

"Jail," Mimi said simply.

Russell took it all back. He'd rather have stuck with not knowing.

"And Michael Brenner?"

"Dead."

Dead? "How?"

"Kylie killed him."

"She what?"

"Hell hath no fury like a woman scorned."

"How? How did she kill him?"

"After he shot you, she whacked him over the head with some sort of ornament and just kept going. They had to identify him via fingerprints. Aurelie tried to get her out of the villa before the cops came, but she refused to leave you." Mimi rolled her eyes as if such sentimentality didn't exist in her world. "So now she's in solitary for her own protection."

Solitary? Solitary confinement would destroy her. Now that Russell had got to know Kylie better, he'd begun to understand what a toll her time alone had taken.

"We need to get her out of there. Does she have a lawyer? I'll hire her a lawyer."

"You think we're not trying? We've already sent a lawyer in. Kylie asks after you and her parents, but apart from that, she just told him to thank us for our help and to inform us it's better we forget about her now."

That obviously wasn't an option. "Can I speak to her? Call her somehow?"

"She's not taking calls."

Oh, Kylie. Sweet, stubborn Kylie. "How are her parents holding up?"

"As well as can be expected. Brenner apparently told her an associate was holding them hostage, but when our team got there, her mother was baking a cake and her father was gardening. We've got someone with them just in case, but Brenner was most likely bluffing. Mulhearn's on the run, and the rest of Brenner's network's either arrested or dead."

"What have the police charged Kylie with?"

"At the moment? Two counts of murder, reckless conduct endangering life and evading police for the motorcycle chase, and possession of an unlicensed firearm."

"That's all bull. And *you* were the one in control of the motorcycle."

"You know that and I know that..."

"You should come clean."

Mimi just laughed. "Give the lawyer a chance. We can get rid of the motorcycle issue, easy. Shane stole a bike to chase us, and at no point did he identify himself as a police officer. Anyone would try to get away if they feared for their fucking life, and I didn't even run any red lights. We can probably get them to drop the Michael shit too. Kylie clearly acted in self-defence."

"Which leaves us with our original problem," Luke said. "The murder of Jasper John."

Back to square one, except with higher stakes since

Kylie was locked away. Russell tried to sit up again, but his muscles wouldn't cooperate. Had they drugged him or something?

"I need to get out of here."

Mimi laughed. "That's funny. They just dug a bullet out of your rib and sewed your chest back together, dude. You're not going anywhere. Do you want your lung to collapse again?"

"But—"

"Forget it. Luke's going to sit here with you while he works, and we'll keep you updated on the other stuff. Get some sleep, okay?"

Sleep? How could he sleep? He'd had quite enough rest while he was unconscious. When the door to the private room clicked shut behind Mimi, he tried to shuffle up the bed, but it felt as though someone was sawing his ribcage in half.

"There's an easier way to do that."

Luke picked up a remote control and aimed it at the bed. Slowly, the top end raised, letting Russell get a better look at the room. White walls, grey carpet, two mint-green chairs, and one of those wheeled tables that fitted over the bed. Nobody had sent flowers.

"High enough?" Luke asked.

"Thanks."

"Do you need more painkillers?"

"It's okay as long as I don't move." Or breathe.

"If it's any consolation, the docs say you were lucky."

"Lucky? Then we've got a very different idea of luck."

"Brenner shot you with his service pistol. Forty calibre. It nicked a front rib, went through the edge of your lung, and lodged in another rib at the back. There's not a lot left of that one, by all accounts. But a couple of inches higher or lower..."

Okay, okay, he got the message. "Can we...?" Geez, it hurt to talk. "Can we focus on the problem at hand? What's happening with the case? How long have I been out?"

"About two days. It's Thursday afternoon."

Two days? Fuck. Russell screwed his eyes shut, trying to remember everything that had happened on Monday, but apart from a vivid picture of Brenner pointing a gun at him, it was hazy.

"I've got a headache."

"I'm not surprised. You've also got a concussion. Brenner knocked you out first, but then you came round and tried to save Kylie."

"I didn't do a very good job of it, did I? My laptops... What happened to my laptops?"

Did the police have them? Russell's own machines were encrypted and had a kill switch that would wipe the hard drives if someone tried to force their way in, but Brenner's laptop was halfway open now. Right before the man arrived, Russell had been digging around in his bank accounts.

"I've got them. Akeem cleared them out of the villa before the old bill arrived."

"Give that man a pat on the back."

"And his boyfriend too. It was him who stopped you from drowning in your own blood."

Sheesh. It'd been a close call, hadn't it? But Russell couldn't afford to dwell on that, not when Kylie was sitting by herself in a cell. He'd heal physically, but if he didn't get her out fast, she'd be left with deeper scars than his.

"I'll send him a crate of beer. Hell, I'll buy him a brewery. Can you put one of my laptops on the table here?"

"You're not seriously considering working?"

"Just do it, would you?"

Luke sighed but got to his feet. A kindred spirit, thank goodness. If the positions had been reversed, Luke would be doing exactly the same, which was to say whatever it took to get the girl he loved out of jail. Yes, Russell loved Kylie. He'd been halfway there before he even kissed her, and now that he'd had a taste of those lips, there was no going back.

Only forward.

The laptops were in a bag beside Luke, three sleek silver machines and Brenner's clunky black box. Luke pulled one of the good ones out.

"Any preferences?"

"They're all the same, and they sync together."

"Good setup. Nice encryption, by the way. I took a look at one of them last night, and it almost tripped me up."

"You didn't fry it, did you?"

"No, I backed off. What's the plan? Where did you get to?"

"We were trying to find leverage over Brenner. I got as far as moving his ill-gotten gains into an offshore account, but that doesn't really matter now. Since I got here, the original case has been on the back burner while we focused on the asshole's more recent crimes. I guess we figured that if we brought him down for those, we could go back and clear Kylie's name afterwards."

"So let's start. What should we look at first?"

They had the police files, Kylie's memories, and Brenner's laptop. Kylie's memories weren't evidence, and from what Russell had seen on Michael's hard drive, he was unlikely to have left a confession on there. The guy was pretty careful when it came to stuff like that. There was no mention of drugs or underworld contacts, and his calendar was written mostly in code. On the day of Jasper John's murder, Michael had left himself a reminder to take out the trash, and that was it.

"The police files. Let's start with the police files."

Chapter 18 - Russ

THE PROBLEM WITH looking at the police files was that Russell felt more at home in cyberspace than the real world. He wasn't a detective, and he almost vomited at the sight of the autopsy pictures. Then regretted it because when the gag reflex hit, it felt like he was bringing up a lung. He'd avoided that part of the report when he downloaded it previously, and with good reason it seemed.

"What are we even looking for?" Luke asked.

"Buggered if I know."

The door cracked open, and a bunch of chrysanthemums poked through the gap. A florist? No, Leyton.

"What's with the bouquet?" Luke asked. "And the fruit basket?"

"Akeem sent them. He wanted to come himself, but he's busy supervising the cleaning crew in Emmy's villa. Apparently, the blood's stained the tile and they might have to replace the whole floor."

Another flashback hit, this time of Brenner's finger twitching on the trigger. Russell grimaced on instinct as he imagined himself lying in the bedroom doorway, sticky red blood pooling around him as Kylie acted to save both of their lives.

"Shit, sorry," Leyton said. "That was insensitive. I'm

no good at the hearts and flowers thing."

Russell attempted a smile. "I'm sure Akeem can train you."

"I guess. How're you feeling?"

"Like I got flattened by a tank, but the doctor said that's normal. Have you seen Kylie? Is she okay?"

Leyton shook his head. "The only person allowed in is the lawyer. Kylie tried to send him away and use a public defender instead, but our guy told her he'd been hired to represent her no matter what, so if she wouldn't speak to him, he'd just sit outside in the hallway until she changed her mind."

"Good. I'll cover his bills."

"You'll have to talk to Mimi about that."

"Mimi? Why Mimi?"

"Because she's the one who hired him, and she is *pissed*. I'm keeping out of her way at the moment."

"She's upset with you?"

"Me, herself, the QPS, security at the hotel, the Feds... The list is endless."

"Why's she upset with you?"

"Because..." Leyton closed his eyes for a second, then scrubbed a hand through already messy hair. He looked more exhausted than Russell felt. "Because it was me Brenner tracked to find you at the resort. He told Kylie."

What? "He followed you?"

"Didn't have to. Once he worked out I was involved, he just zeroed in on my phone. As a cop, he had access to tracking data, and nobody at the QPS thought to shut it off after he went rogue. I'm sorry, mate. I don't know what else to say."

Russell hadn't even considered how Brenner had

found them, which said a lot about his abilities as a detective. For a second, he felt angry at Leyton too because working these things out was his job, but he quickly forced that prickly little ball of animosity out of the picture where it belonged. Perhaps with a crystal ball, they could have foreseen Brenner coming for Kylie, but he should've been halfway to Kuala Lumpur by that point. Getting upset with Leyton wouldn't further Kylie's cause in the slightest.

"What's done is done. I'll live, but it won't be much of a life if Kylie's stuck in prison."

Leyton's eyebrows shot up into his hairline. "I thought all that marriage stuff was just a pretence."

"It was, and then it wasn't."

The two men stared at Russell.

"Uh, congratulations?" Luke offered.

"Can we just focus on getting her out of prison?"

Leyton's shoulders dropped an inch. "Too right we can. And if we can't do it legally, Mimi'll bust her out." From his tone, he was only half-joking. "I need to read through the police file again, right from the start. I suggest you two do the same—people tend to spot different things."

"What are we looking for?"

"Leads to our possible witness, forensic anomalies, anything that doesn't feel right. That doesn't fit. Nobody gets away clean, but sometimes the clues are hard to spot."

Luke got out a third laptop, Leyton pulled up an ugly green chair, and they clustered around the wheeled table. Jasper John had died in his kitchen, sprawled face down on the cracked linoleum with a bullet hole in the back of his head. An exit wound, according to the autopsy report. He'd actually been shot twice, but one of the rounds had still been rattling around inside his skull. By the looks of it, he'd died in the middle of making dinner. A pot of pasta sat on the stove, and half a pepper lay on the chopping board beside a knife. He hadn't been afraid when he died. Whoever shot him had caught him by surprise, because otherwise, he'd have grabbed the knife to defend himself, surely?

"They found a number of unidentified fingerprints in the house," Luke said.

"They did," Leyton agreed. "We got a friendly contact to run them through NAFIS, but there weren't any new hits. Whoever left them either never committed a crime, or they were too smart to get caught. And there was nothing from Brenner. He must've worn gloves."

"Playing devil's advocate here, but are we sure he did it? John wasn't exactly squeaky clean. They found a large quantity of cannabis in the spare bedroom."

"Brenner admitted as much to Kylie. Basically told her it was her fault for being stupid enough to get framed."

While Russell hated the fact that Kylie had killed Brenner, he was glad the man was dead. His only regret? That it hadn't been more painful. The tension radiating through him made his ribs hurt, and he forced himself to relax. To take deeper breaths and ignore the ribbons of pain that sliced through his chest. *Focus on the evidence, Weisz.*

Jasper John had been a small man, five feet six maybe, his haircut bordering on a mullet and his clothes on the loose side of relaxed fit. A size too big, possibly two. Had he been on a diet? A box on the counter had a picture of fruit on the side, and Russell zoomed in. FatBuster weight loss shakes. Yes, a diet. He squinted at the picture again. Something wasn't right with it, but what? A thought niggled, but thinking made his head throb.

"What time did he die?" Luke asked Leyton.

"From the liver temperature, between seven and seven thirty."

"And the emergency call was made at, uh, seven thirty-two. Fits."

Luke chewed the end of a pen. Did he keep it for that very purpose? Russell had certainly never seen him write anything by hand.

"Scruffy guy," he muttered absentmindedly.

"Yet he seemed hot on personal hygiene," Leyton said. "There's a note on the autopsy report that he smelled strongly of cologne and either breath mints or toothpaste."

That was it! The truth hit Russell like a nuclear blast. Unfortunately. He gasped for breath, and his chest spasmed. He would have doubled up in pain if his muscles had cooperated.

"I'll call the nurse." Leyton scrambled for the remote control and jabbed at the buttons. "Get you some painkillers. Can you breathe? Is something bleeding? We need a doctor."

He got halfway to the door before Russell managed to raise a hand. "Stop."

"What?"

"The pot. Look...look at the pot."

"Pot?" Luke scrolled through whatever report he was reading. "There was three kilos of it, plus a small quantity of cocaine and some Xanax. But I haven't seen any pictures."

"No, the pot on the stove. The pasta."

"He was making dinner. So what?"

"Dinner for two. John was counting calories, and that's way too much pasta for one person."

"It is?"

"Yes, it is. Trust me—I only know how to cook three things, and spaghetti's one of them." Plus Russell knew the joys of dieting. Nobody serious about losing weight would load up on pasta like that. The pain came again, more intense this time, and he bunched the sheets up in his fists as beads of sweat popped out all over his body. "John was...he was...he was making a meal for two."

Leyton thumped a fist on the table. "That's it! That's what we've been missing. The witness wasn't a passer-by. She was in the damn house."

"Who was she?" Luke asked. "A girlfriend? Why didn't she come forward?"

Russell didn't have time to contemplate the question before a nurse rushed in, took one look at him, and called for the doctor.

"What are these computers doing in here? You shouldn't be playing games."

Russell had managed to switch to his emergency screensaver, a recording of *The Sims*, but that didn't appease her.

"Put all this stuff away." She glared at Luke and Leyton. "You two should be ashamed of yourselves. Mr. Weisz had a major operation the day before yesterday."

"I'm...I'm fine."

"No, Mr Weisz, you're not fine. You need to rest."

"But—"

The doctor arrived and stuck him with a needle, the sting followed by a glorious numbness that allowed Russell to breathe again. But the man shared the nurse's attitude.

"You gentlemen need to leave, I'm afraid. Let's focus on keeping Mr. Weisz alive rather than his avatar, eh?"

Luke tucked one of Russell's laptops into a bag and left it on the chair beside the bed, then he and Leyton packed up the rest of the equipment and backed out of the room under the watchful gaze of the nurse. She didn't look like a woman to mess with, and truth be told, Russell was exhausted.

"We'll be back later," Leyton muttered as the door closed.

Could they be right? Had Jasper John had a woman in the house when he got shot? The place had been a tip —dust bunnies in every corner, dirty streaks all over the bathroom, men's clothes scattered on the floor in the bedroom. Utterly devoid of a female touch. If Russell's home looked like that, he'd have been mortally embarrassed had a lady walked in. Was it really possible John had a girlfriend? Surely if he wanted to impress a date, he'd have taken her out to a restaurant? Russell began to second-guess himself. Perhaps the man had just had a craving for carbs?

Then the questions faded away, and Russell saw Kylie again, walking towards him on the beach wearing that tiny green bikini. The one that made him want to drag her into his arms and keep her there for good. He should have done that. Should have chartered a flight to Morocco and gotten the hell out of Australia as soon as Brenner got away. Why hadn't he?

Should have, should have, should have...

Chapter 19 - Mimi

MIMI TRAN CAME back down to earth with a bump.

Quite literally.

A little hop-skip, and she bundled her parachute into her arms and turned to look for her jump buddy. Dontae was right behind her, already jogging. BASE jumping was frowned upon—okay, it was illegal—in Brisbane, and the security guard at the construction site whose crane they'd borrowed had probably called the cops already.

Just after sunrise, the central business district was barely stirring, which gave them a clear run to Dontae's truck, parked neatly on a side street. The first siren sounded as she opened the passenger door, and only once he'd started the engine did she allow herself to smile a rare natural smile.

"That went well."

"Bitch, you're crazy."

Okay, perhaps she should've deployed her chute a second or two sooner, but what was life without a touch of danger? Adrenaline was her drug of choice, although coke would certainly be easier to obtain. She mentally rolled her eyes as she thought of the bust at the pizzeria earlier in the week. Home fucking delivery.

"Still breathing, aren't I?"

"You're like a damn cat. Nine lives, and you always

land the right way up."

Not to mention the sharp claws. "Miaow."

"Where do you want me to drop you? Home?"

Dontae was one of the few people who knew where she lived, but she shook her head. "The office."

"Busy day?"

"Busy life." Dontae was a friend—or as close to a friend as Mimi had—but they never discussed her work. Maybe that was why she liked him? Because he broke the law but didn't try to break down the walls she'd constructed around herself? No, not walls. More of a nuclear fallout shelter. "You?"

"People's lawns won't mow themselves."

They wouldn't. For three months after Maynard died, Mimi had mowed the lawn herself, cursing the entire time because she hated the pointlessness of it. The grass never stopped growing. She'd been on the verge of concreting the whole bloody lot when she bumped into Dontae at the top of Wallaman Falls early one September morning. They'd bonded over a shared love of heights, and now he tidied up her garden every week and took care of the cat when she was away.

While Dontae drove, Mimi stripped off her body armour and helmet. She'd pack up her parachute, a seven-cell ram-air with a specially modified slider, later. The table in the big conference room at Blackwood made the perfect spot for that.

"Stopping for coffee?" Dontae asked.

"Why ask when you already know the answer?"

He slowed to a halt outside her favourite coffee place, not one of the big chains but a blink-and-you'd-miss-it hole-in-the-wall run by three brothers. Two minutes later, she was back in the truck with a plain black coffee for her; a latte with caramel syrup for Dontae; plus a cappuccino for Merindah, her assistant, and five minutes after that, they pulled up outside Blackwood's building.

"Same time next week?" Dontae asked.

"Find us somewhere to jump, and I'm there."

She took the steps two at a time and paused in front of the retina scanner. A quiet click, and the door slid open. Not for the first time, she mused over how strange it was to have an almost legitimate job. Ten years in the shadows had left her marvelling at the small things—a receptionist who greeted her by name, colleagues who brought in cakes on their birthdays, a desk with a motherfucking plant.

Oh, and meetings. Who could forget the endless meetings?

"Leyton's in meeting room four," her assistant called the second she walked through the door on the third floor.

Early for him. Rix was more of a night owl. Which meant it was probably important, which meant she should probably go see him before she repacked her parachute. She dumped Merindah's coffee on her desk then held out the bundle of fabric.

"Could you please put this in the conference room?" *Smile, Mimi.* Even after so many years, the expression felt forced, and she had to remind her lips to move. Politeness was an act with her. A part she played out of necessity. "Thank you."

In meeting room four, Rix was slumped in a chair with the English geek beside him. One of Emmy's people—and also her ex, apparently. Mimi couldn't imagine Emmy dating a guy like that, but she said she hadn't been in her right mind at the time.

"Yes?" she asked, perching on the edge of the table. The coffee had cooled now, but caffeine was caffeine. She took another mouthful. "Did you find something?"

They must have, or they wouldn't have called her. Mimi didn't normally get involved with cases like this, the mundane stuff, but this one was important to Emmy, and so there she was.

"We questioned Jasper John's neighbours again yesterday afternoon, the ones who were home, at any rate," Rix said. "We're working on the theory that he might have had a girlfriend, and there's a possibility she might have been the one to make the emergency call."

"Why do you think that?"

"According to the ME, John's mouth smelled minty fresh, and he'd doused himself with aftershave. No man does that if he plans to sit at home alone. Plus he was cooking enough dinner for two."

Mimi wrinkled her nose. "His house was disgusting. I'd need to get paid to go in there."

Rix stared at her. Like, properly stared. What was wrong with him? Was he having a fucking seizure? She reached out to poke him, then remembered Maynard's training. *Manners, Mimi.*

"Are you okay?"

"What if that's it? What if he was paying her?"

Luke nodded, his eyes coming alive. "It fits. That woman with the yappy dog said the girl she saw was pretty, too pretty for John, but she always dressed cheap."

"Young ladies should be more modest," Rix mimicked, his voice high-pitched. "There's nothing wrong with a skirt below the knees."

Bullshit. There was everything wrong with a skirt below the knees. You couldn't run, you couldn't jump... Sure, it gave a girl somewhere to hide a gun, but a loose sweater was ten times better.

"Is that all you have on her?" Mimi asked. "Trashy dresser?"

"Long brown hair, always worn loose, fine features, too thin. Favoured high heels and never smiled. We're gonna go back and try the other neighbours, see if anyone else remembers her."

"Keep me updated. Any news on Kylie? Has she come to her senses yet?"

Mimi asked because it was expected of her. Sympathy wasn't one of her strong points. But secretly, she empathised with Kylie more than she'd ever let on to her colleagues. Only Emmy and a few shadowy government officials had ever known the truth about Mimi's past, and like Maynard, most of them were dead now. People in Section Zero didn't have a long life expectancy.

"Nope. Her lawyer says she's shut down. Says she's a lost cause."

Mimi had once thought that about herself. Perhaps she should give Maynard's successor at Zero a nudge, see if he needed a new recruit? Actually, no. Kylie was good in a crisis, by all accounts, but she was too damn nice to dispose of people on a regular basis. And nervy. She'd never handle the pressure. Besides, she wasn't alone, not the way Mimi had been. Kylie had the whole of Blackwood looking out for her.

"No point in wasting time trying to convince her otherwise. Get people out on the street to look for this brunette instead."

"Are you busy today?"

"I am now. I'll call if I find anything."

A sex worker... Where to start? The men would take the streets. It was the obvious place to start, but none of the girls would be out till later. How about *their* girl? They were talking three years ago, and not many lasted that long in the sex industry. The lucky few turned their lives around and went straight, while others were lost to drugs or illness or occasionally murder.

Mimi was the exception to the rule, she supposed. She'd lasted ten months, and her escape hadn't been so much of a dash to freedom as a slow descent into hell. Fucking Maynard. She still missed the old guy.

Her BMW was in the underground parking garage, right where she'd left it about a week ago. Most of the time, she preferred her bike, a sleek black Honda, but she tended to take a car when she visited the women's shelter. Sometimes she needed to run an errand or give one of the girls a ride somewhere.

Jasmine House was an unassuming three-storey building, a former office block converted into studio apartments, temporary homes for women who needed a helping hand. The old conference rooms had become a lounge and communal dining area, and the ground floor housed a small gym as well as the staff offices. There was always at least one resident advocate on hand to assist. The RAs answered the phone and provided counselling and support so the girls didn't feel alone at what was a pretty shitty point in their lives.

Mimi had bought the building with money she liberated from a sex trafficker two years previously, and she paid the RA's salaries out of the money she made at Blackwood.

Around half of the residents used to work in the sex industry, so she figured it'd be a good place to start in the search for Jasper John's female friend.

The management team tried hard not to let Jasmine House feel like what it was—a last resort for many of the women. They'd painted the lobby a calming magnolia, scattered comfortable seats around a coffee machine, and a forest of greenery let in dappled light while discouraging prying eyes. A young blonde was curled up on one of the sofas with a novel when Mimi let herself in.

"Hey, is Annalise around?"

"She's talking to a new girl. They might be a while, I think. Thanks for bringing more books." She held up the one she was reading. "I'm halfway through already. And also the phone. I haven't called anyone yet, but..."

"There's no hurry." Sally's last phone had come to a nasty end when Mimi threw it at her former pimp. Broke his nose. Promised to break his teeth too if he tried coming after Sally. "I'm actually looking for a girl. She may have been in the industry three or four years ago, working around Durack."

"Is she in trouble?"

"Not at all, but she might have witnessed a crime back then, and I need to find out if she knows anything."

"What crime?"

Mimi hesitated. She didn't want to bring darkness into this place, but then she thought of Kylie sitting in a ten-by-twelve box flooded with artificial light.

"A murder. Somebody else got the blame, but she was set up, and I'm trying to clear her name."

Sally's eyes widened. "A murder? Who died?"

"A man called Jasper John. He dealt cannabis and ran a poker game at Mikey's bar over in Inala."

"The guy on the news? They said a cop shot him." Sally's eyes bugged out again. "That's who you're trying to clear? The cop? She killed another guy too. Strangled him with her bare hands—that's what they're saying."

"Everything they say on TV is bullshit. She's not a cold-blooded killer."

No, that was Mimi. The more she thought about it, the more the idea of Kylie Nichols raising a silenced pistol to a man's head and pulling the trigger without flinching was laughable.

Sally put down the paperback and thought for a moment, chewing her lip. "Last year, the police said my friend Beth murdered her ex, but no way did she do that. He tried to rape her, and it wasn't the first time. How can pushing someone down the stairs in self-defence be murder?"

"What happened to her?"

"She OD'd before the trial."

Fuck. "I don't want anyone else to die."

Not in this particular case, anyway. Well, apart from Owen Mills. Mimi had already checked out his room at the hospital. Sure, there was a police guard outside, but that was just a minor inconvenience.

"I think Marilyn worked in Durack," Sally said. "She was eating breakfast twenty minutes ago. You know her?"

"I know her."

"Wait, I'll come with you. This is kind of exciting, huh? Playing detective?"

Some days, Mimi woke up wanting to right every wrong in the world. Other days, she didn't want to get out of bed at all. But she'd tried retiring and got bored after six weeks, so what did that leave? She wasn't cut out for a desk job.

"Right. Kind of exciting."

Chapter 20 - Mimi

WHEN SALLY EXPLAINED the situation to Marilyn, half a dozen other girls listened in, and by the time Mimi finished her cup of coffee, they were already calling their friends and acquaintances with the mystery woman's description. Two hours later, Mimi had sat in on a self-defence class run by one of their few male volunteers, caught up on her emails, scheduled a hostage rescue simulation for her team, and ordered cat treats on the internet.

Mimi headed up the Australian branch of Emmy Black's Special Projects division. They handled all the shit that nobody else in Blackwood wanted to touch. For years, Emmy had overseen everything herself, but with business booming and Australia such a long flight away from her US base, she'd brought Mimi on board to help out.

An experiment in delegation, she'd called it to start with. If it didn't work out, they'd agreed to part company, no hard feelings, but a year and a half on, Mimi was enjoying her new role more than she thought she would. Being able to pick and choose her jobs was an improvement over being forced to accept orders she often disagreed with, and Emmy had become a friend. It was nice being able to pick up the phone and talk with someone who *understood*.

Movement by the door of the dining room caught Mimi's eye, and she looked up to find Sally approaching with what seemed like half of the residents in tow. A delegation.

"Her name's Bayley," Sally said. "With a *Y* in the middle." She looked around at the others. "We think so, anyway, don't we?"

Murmurs of agreement came from all sides.

"Can you start from the beginning? Please?"

"One of Sammi's friends thought she remembered a real skinny girl who used to work in that area. Hung out by Mikey's."

"She ran away from home, my friend thought," Sammi piped up. "Always seemed nervous."

"Never really fitted in," another girl said. "Like she came from a good family and took a wrong turn."

"Is she still around? Does anyone know how to find her?"

"Nah, we spoke to her old roommate, and she disappeared right after that guy got shot."

"Disappeared?"

Mimi had visions of another body, this time young and female.

"Not like that. She said she was getting out of the business, that she'd had enough."

"Did she say what she was going to do instead?"

A shrug. "Not really."

"Do you think her roommate would talk to me?"

"Yeah, I told Kirsty you were okay, and she said she'll be home until twelve, then she's got to go to her waitressing job."

Mimi wrote her address down, promised to visit again soon, and jogged out to her car. Could Bayley-with-a-Y be the breakthrough they were looking for?

"Sorry about the mess," Kirsty said, swinging the door open wider once Mimi had explained who she was and why she was there. "Laurie said you might come over, but I'm not sure I can help much. I haven't seen Bayley in three years."

Mimi glanced around the place. The mess didn't come so much from untidiness, more from peeling wallpaper and a stained carpet. The outside of the apartment building wasn't much better. Kirsty herself took care over her appearance—her red hair was tied back in a high ponytail, and her manicure looked fresh. But her eyes were tired.

"At the moment, we know next to nothing about her. She lived here with you? Or somewhere else?"

"Yes, here for six months, but she mostly kept to herself. I used to hear her crying at night, but she never wanted to discuss it, you know?"

"Why do *you* think she cried?"

"Honestly, she never said much. She was always so quiet. Most of the time, I didn't even know she was here."

"But if you had to guess... Was she upset over the present or the past?"

Kirsty picked at her bracelet, a cheap gold chain with plastic charms dangling from it. "Both, I guess. She told me her dad died."

"Anything else about her family?"

"Not much. I think she had a brother, but he never visited. Thinking back, she hardly ever socialised. She seemed to prefer being on her own."

"No boyfriend?"

"Not that I saw." The catch on the bracelet broke, and it fell to the floor. "Dammit. You know what line of work we were in?"

"Yes."

"Then you'll know that being single wasn't exactly unusual. There aren't many guys who'll date a girl who sleeps with assholes for money."

"Did Laurie tell you much about why I'm here?"

"Not really. Just that you're looking for Bayley as a witness to a crime, and I should talk to you because you're a good person."

A good person? Mimi turned her snort of laughter into a cough. Well, that just went to show how perceptions could differ. Not many "good people" had body counts in triple figures.

"Rumour has it that Bayley may have had dinner with a murder victim right before he died."

"Dinner?" For a moment, Kirsty frowned, puzzled. But then her forehead smoothed out. "Was it a Friday? It was a Friday, right?"

Was it? Mimi had to get her phone out and scroll back three years in her calendar to check. This was why Rix was the detective and she was the assassin. Rix would have known that detail right away.

"Uh, yes. A Friday."

"That was the Friday-night foodie. At least, that's what Bayley used to call him. He always paid her for the whole evening, but he insisted on cooking her dinner and watching TV instead of...you know. She reckoned he couldn't get it up. Lonely old guy, just liked the company, probably. When she first started going over to his place, she told me about him. Wanted to know if that sort of arrangement was normal."

"And what did you tell her?"

"That it definitely wasn't normal, but if she could make that kind of cash by talking instead of fucking, she should go for it."

"She saw him every week?"

"I don't know for sure, but I think most weeks. She always dressed up nice, and I never saw her for the rest of the evening. We used to work the same area, so I used to see her around most nights when we were out."

"But she quit?"

"Yeah, about three years ago."

"Can you give me an approximate date?"

"Sorry." A shrug. "Bad memory."

"Was it summer or winter?"

"Uh…" Kirsty's mouth bunched up as she thought. "Summer? When she left, I had to find someone to take her room, and nobody wanted it because the AC was broken."

That fitted. Jasper John had croaked in February.

"Did she say anything about her future plans? Did she get a new job?"

"I don't think so. It was sudden, her decision. She seemed really nervous for a week or so, then she said she was leaving."

Nervous over having witnessed a murder? "Any idea what scared her?"

"We almost got busted. One minute, we were hanging around, waiting for customers, and the next, there were cops everywhere. We had to run, and she twisted an ankle. It puffed up huge and went all yellow. Looked like a cantaloupe."

"Was that before or after...?" Mimi gave herself a mental kick. Asking whether the bust was before or after the murder was pointless when Kirsty didn't know Jasper John and barely even remembered the season. "And you're sure she didn't say where she was going?"

"Not really. She said she wanted to see the world, and that was it. I thought she'd be back after a few weeks when she worked out how much travelling cost, but she never came."

"Why did you think she'd come back here? Did she pay rent up front?"

"She gave me a month in lieu of notice, but she left a box of her stuff here. Asked me to keep it safe until she collected it."

Mimi's ears pricked up. "A box of her stuff? Do you still have it?"

"In my closet. But some of it got damaged when the roof leaked."

They had her. Bayley *had* to be the girl they were looking for; Mimi was sure of it. All the pieces fitted together. But now they had to find her.

"Can I take a look?"

"Don't see why not. It's not like she wants it. Can you do me a favour? If you find her, tell her I need my closet space back."

"Her name's Hanna Pearson."

Mimi dropped Hanna's library card onto the table over Russell's hospital bed, complete with her photo on the back. She'd been pretty in a gaunt sort of way. Good teeth, but even though she was smiling, her eyes looked sad.

Mimi had stopped at the library on the way back and used a self-service kiosk to check Hanna's borrowing history. She'd last used the card two days before Jasper John's murder, and she'd run up hundreds of dollars in fines for the three books she hadn't returned. Two thrillers, one romance. Until then, she'd visited the library once a week, regular as clockwork, a voracious reader getting her fix. Mimi had dropped a hundred dollars into the donations box on her way out—enough to cover the cost of the missing paperbacks. Reading was important, and as a young child, all of her books had come from the library. Her mama had worked hard, but money was always too tight to buy anything but the essentials.

Russell looked like shit, which was only to be expected, but he sat up a little straighter with the news. Then winced. Mimi had never been shot in the lung, just the leg and an arm, but bullets hurt like a bitch. Probably she should've brought a box of chocolates or something, feigned sympathy, but Akeem seemed to have turned the room into a fucking jungle and there wasn't room for so much as a card.

"Hanna Pearson? Are you sure?" Rix asked.

"Of course I'm fucking sure. Otherwise I'd have included a qualifier with that."

A "might" or a "maybe." Duh.

"How did you get her name?"

"Talked to people."

"Where is she?"

"If I had all the answers, you'd be out of a job, Detective Rix. Apparently, she went travelling, so she could be anywhere."

Russell was already typing. Give the boy a gold star for effort.

"Can I see that library card?" he asked.

Rix slid it over, and Russell studied it for a second.

"She's in Mexico."

Everyone stared at him.

"How'd you find that out?" Mimi asked.

"Facebook."

Fucking Facebook. Mimi burst out laughing, and now everyone stared at her. She quickly arranged her features into a scowl as Russell turned his laptop around.

"She joined six months ago. I guess she thought it was safe by then."

Figured. After Kylie ran, the Jasper John case went quiet, and there'd never been a comprehensive search for Hanna let alone a request that would warrant her extradition as a witness. After two and a half years of lying low, dipping a toe into social media didn't seem like an outlandish thing for her to do.

And the pictures on the Facebook profile did bear a strong resemblance to the girl on the library card. The hair was different, but that was a triviality. Mimi had to agree with Russell's assessment that they were the same person.

"How do you know she's in Mexico? There's no location on her posts."

Russell scrolled down the feed. "No, but see here? She took a picture of a street artist, and unless I'm very much mistaken, the building in the background is the church of Santo Domingo de Guzmán in Oaxaca. My brother travelled around Mexico before he moved to Egypt, and that was one of the places he visited. It's part of an eighteenth-century monastery."

Luke held up a Wikipedia entry on his phone. "He's right. It's the same building."

Mimi had to admit that technology had its uses, although she still favoured human intelligence. And it didn't really surprise her that Russell was a history buff.

"So, Hanna's in Mexico. Then I guess someone needs to go and fetch her."

CHAPTER 21 - KYLIE

"YOUR LAWYER'S HERE. Hands out."

I'd been in jail for exactly two weeks, and apart from a brief court hearing where I confirmed my name and lack of address, three cold showers, and the uncomfortable meetings with Jarrod Fulton, my Blackwood-appointed lawyer, I hadn't left my cell. My blood-covered bathrobe had been exchanged for prison greens, already too big because I'd barely eaten, and sleepless nights meant I knew every crack on the ceiling, every smudge on the wall.

I'd also become well-acquainted with my own mind. The fear and the guilt. If I could've turned back the clock three years, I'd have walked into Superintendent Clarke's office and handwritten a confession. Not because of what happened to Michael, Shane, and Owen—they deserved everything they got, even if Michael's bloodied face did haunt my nightmares—but because of Russell. He'd been shot because of me. He'd almost *died*.

Jarrod said Russell had been rushed into surgery, that a bullet had been removed from his chest but he was recovering now. Each time I asked how bad it was, Jarrod glossed over the details. Which meant it was seriously bad. But as long as Russell was alive... The updates on him were the only reason I spoke to Jarrod at all. I didn't want Blackwood's assistance anymore. They'd done nothing but help me, and in return, I'd turned people's lives upside down. Far easier to accept my fate. Living in a cell was preferable to living with the knowledge that another person I cared about had been injured.

"Okay," I told the guard, then held my hands ready for cuffing.

When I first arrived, the guards had glared at me like I was some kind of monster. The cop killer. They looked out for their own, and I still had the bruises to prove it. But I didn't complain. What was the point? The glares gradually subsided, replaced by scowls and barked orders. In their position, I probably wouldn't have liked me much either, so I couldn't blame them for their attitudes. They didn't have all the facts. They were just doing their jobs as I'd tried to do mine.

Click. The cuffs went on.

For past visits, they'd led me into a room smaller than my cell, bare except for a metal table and chairs, but this time, I was shown into a bigger room. No table. No chairs. What was going on?

"Why is she wearing handcuffs?" Jarrod snapped. "Take them off."

Well, this was different.

I thought the guard might argue—he looked as if he wanted to—but he complied. Words were muttered as I rubbed some feeling back into my wrists, then Jarrod guided me towards another door with a hand on the small of my back.

"What's happening?" I whispered.

"They're just finishing up the paperwork, and then you're free to go."

I stopped mid-stride. "What?"

"Unless you want to stay?" Jarrod smiled, but it didn't really fit his face. He'd always struck me as Mr. Gravitas. Kind but oh-so-serious. "Though I don't recommend that." He pushed another door open. "Keep your head down."

"What?"

My vocabulary was sorely lacking. I only had one word left.

"Keep your head down."

I didn't have time to process that or ask further questions before the flashes hit me. There must've been a hundred people taking pictures as Jarrod bundled me through the crowd and into a waiting car. I couldn't see properly anymore. The bright lights seared into my retinas, leaving me blinded. People called my name, shouting questions I couldn't understand since they were all yelling at the same time.

"Hey."

Oh my gosh. *I knew that voice.*

I blinked furiously, trying to clear my vision, and Russell's blurry form appeared in front of me. Was this a dream? Was I even awake? I reached out for him, but he held up a hand.

"Careful. I'm a bit bashed up."

He was there? He was truly there? Someone slammed the car door, and tears rolled down my cheeks as people started banging on the blacked-out windows. Jarrod climbed into the front and ordered the man behind the wheel to drive.

"You came?" I said. "You really came?"

"How many times do I have to tell you? I don't do flings."

My heart swelled up so big I thought it would burst out of my ribcage, which would've been awful because one person with a chest injury was quite bad enough. As the car pulled away, I scrambled up onto the seat and straddled Russell, careful not to touch any part of his torso.

"You came." I cupped his cheeks in my hands and kissed him, a wild clash of tongues and teeth that left me breathless. "You came."

"Of course I did. I love you."

How did I have any tears left in me? I laid my forehead against his. "I love you too. So, so much. But I don't understand—how am *I* here? What happened?"

"That, darling, is a long, long story. It's probably best if we tell it over dinner."

"Dinner?"

"At the Black Diamond. Apparently, Akeem's already replaced the floor in Emmy's villa and patched up the bullet hole."

The bullet hole in the floor. Yet another reminder of my failures, but not nearly as bad as the hole in Russ's chest. That... That made my own insides seize every time I thought about it, which over the past two weeks had been every waking minute of every day, and most of the nights too.

"Are you okay? I thought you were dead, I—"

He kissed me again. "Don't think about it. The doctors say I'll be as good as new in a few months."

Don't think about it? How could I not? "Is Emmy really mad about the damage?"

"Not in the slightest. I offered to pay for the repairs, but she said it was worth every penny. So, what do you say? Dinner?"

Dinner. He tossed the word out casually, as if he hadn't just picked me up from freaking prison. I almost choked on the stupid lump in my throat. Did he honestly have to ask? There was only ever going to be one answer.

"I don't care where I go as long as I'm with you."

When we arrived back at the resort, Jarrod opened the car door for us, and I helped Russell out carefully, lending him my arm. He was putting a brave face on things, but I'd seen the way he winced every time the car went over a bump.

"Shouldn't you still be in the hospital?" I asked.

"I've got painkillers."

That wasn't a proper answer, but Russell was stubborn. If he didn't want to go back there, he wouldn't. I wrapped his arm over my shoulders and supported his weight as we walked slowly up the path to the villa, inhaling in the sweet aroma of the plumeria with a newfound appreciation. I wasn't sure how I felt about going back to the place where my world had fallen apart for the second time just two weeks ago, but Russell wanted to, and I was in no position to object.

Dazed. I was still dazed when we walked through the door, and for some reason, it hadn't occurred to me that the villa would be full of people. Akeem, maybe, but not everyone else. Leyton was there, and Mimi, plus Emmy, Luke, Akeem, Glenn, Aurelie, and a brown-haired girl I'd never seen before. Who was she? Her nervous smile seemed out of place among the celebrations. But I soon forgot to ask when Akeem cheered, threw confetti over us, then popped open an enormous bottle of champagne. Emmy caught the cork in midair.

"How was traffic?" she asked. "We weren't expecting you back for at least half an hour."

Traffic? I had no idea? I'd barely looked out of the window on the journey, content just to sit next to Russell and hold his hand. Grounding myself after everything had been so up-in-the-air.

"Not too bad," Jarrod said from behind me. "The authorities finally got the message about moving quickly, so the paperwork was done when I arrived for the most part."

"Drink?" Akeem asked, holding out two glasses of champagne.

Russell shook his head. "I can't, not with the medication."

Akeem passed them both to me instead. "Then you'll have to drink his. Come on, sit down. You know everyone, right? Well, except for Hanna. *Nobody* knew her until last Friday."

Hanna? That was the brunette? "Uh, hi."

She gave me a little wave. Why did she look so nervous?

"Are you okay?" I asked Russell. "Do you need to lie down?"

"I've done nothing but lie down for the last fortnight, so it feels weirdly good to stand. The painkillers are holding their own at the moment."

"Just say if you want to leave. I guess. I mean, I have no idea where we can go." Presumably since Emmy was there, she'd want her villa back.

"We're in the honeymoon suite tonight." Russell

grinned, which made me smile too. "Akeem's already moved our stuff."

"The honeymoon suite? Are you trying to tell me something?" I tried out a joke, and it felt good.

"Give me a chance to buy a ring first, darling," he murmured. "I'm not asking you without one."

Now he was joking too. Right? Uh, he didn't look like he was joking.

"Will you two sit down, for fuck's sake?" Emmy said. "We've got a lot to catch up on, and I'm hungry."

Akeem just couldn't help himself. "So, after you got dragged off to jail, Luke and Leyton followed Russell to the hospital, and they had this, like, hackers convention until the nurses got upset and kicked them out, and—"

"Akeem, slow down," Emmy told him. "Can you check on the canapés? With the amount of alcohol I plan on drinking tonight, I need something to line my stomach."

"Actually, that's a good idea. Nobody wants to clean up vomit at three o'clock in the morning."

Russell lowered himself onto a seat, and I shuffled mine closer so our legs touched. I never wanted to be away from him again, not even for a second. Akeem vanished out of the door, and Emmy took up the tale.

"As Akeem was saying, the guys convened at the hospital to go through all the evidence from the Jasper John case again. Between them, they worked out there might have been a second person in his house that night. A woman."

A woman? Was that Hanna? I closed my eyes for a second and tried to imagine it. Hanna dating Jasper John? No, it didn't work.

"And they realised he might have paid for that

woman's company."

Oh. *Oh*. Hanna was a prostitute? That made much more sense. I stared at her for a beat too long, and she lowered her gaze to the table.

"Mimi asked around and worked out who she was, and we found her in Oaxaca. She'd been hiding from Michael too, in case he realised she was the witness, but when she found out he was dead, she agreed to come back to Australia and tell her story."

"It was you who called triple zero that night?" I asked.

She spoke for the first time, her voice soft. "Yes. I'm sorry I didn't come forward sooner, but I was so freaked out. I didn't know what to do but run."

Well, we had that much in common. "That I can understand. What did you see?"

It must have been something big or I wouldn't have been sitting there without so much as a trial.

"Jasper wasn't like my regular clients. He used to make dinner for me, and he liked to talk. Most Friday evenings, we got together, and sometimes I stayed the night and he made me breakfast too. I wasn't supposed to be there the night he died. He'd called earlier in the week and said he needed to meet someone, that it was important. I guess that was you?"

"Yes, but he never showed up."

"He said you sent a text message cancelling."

Huh? "I didn't send a message."

"We checked with the phone company," Luke said. "Someone sent a message from your number to John's on the Friday afternoon."

Michael. It must have been Michael. What did he do, delete it afterwards? He could've deleted it from

John's phone too since he'd been at the bloody crime scene.

Emmy followed my train of thought. "I think we can probably guess who did it."

Yup. Everyone nodded.

"Anyhow, Jasper called me and said he was free after all, so I went over," Hanna said. "Except right after I got there, someone knocked on the door. Jasper told me to make myself scarce. I guess he was protecting me, because a man walked right in and shot him. I didn't know who he was at the time, but I saw him on TV afterwards, and he was a cop."

"You saw his face at the house?"

"I was upstairs, and I peeped around the corner just as he looked back towards the kitchen. I couldn't breathe, I was so terrified." Even now, her breath came in little gasps. "But then I heard the door slam, and I ran to help Jasper, but his eyes were just staring... So I hid again and called triple zero, and then I ran."

"And that was why the police let me go? Because you identified Michael? I'm surprised Superintendent Clarke didn't try to say I'd paid you off or something."

"Oh, it gets better," Emmy said. "He did try to claim that, but Hanna here tried to do her civic duty three years ago and mailed him a letter identifying Michael as the shooter right before she left for Thailand."

"Surely he'd have said it got lost in the mail?"

"He did. But she marked it private and confidential, sent it by registered post, and he signed for it. At best, the now ex-Superintendent Clarke was guilty of negligence, and at worst, he was complicit in whatever scheme Brenner had cooked up."

"Oh my gosh. He got fired?"

"Indeed he did. Left the building carrying all the shit off his desk in a box."

"Wow."

"You haven't heard my absolute favourite part yet. The QPS asked if you wanted your old job back. We told them to fuck off on your behalf."

Once I'd loved working there, and a tiny part of me wondered what it would be like to return. But then I remembered that nobody had stuck up for me after the accusations. Not one of my former colleagues had said, "Hold on, that seems out of character." They'd just kept their heads down, more interested in looking after their own interests than getting justice.

"Thank you."

"You're welcome."

While I was away, I'd worked as a freelance graphic artist. I could do that again until I found a new career path. It didn't pay big bucks, but it paid enough. I'd be okay.

And that was it. The nightmare was over. Russell's injury stopped me from whooping with joy, but I did manage a relieved smile as I picked up my glass of champagne.

"I'd like to propose a toast. To the best set of friends a girl could hope to have."

Everyone held their glasses up except for Akeem, who'd just walked back in the door and held up a bottle.

"Cheers."

CHAPTER 22 - KYLIE

RUSSELL DIDN'T MAKE it to three o'clock in the morning. It was eleven when he started looking uncomfortable, and I wasn't about to stay at the party without him. Akeem dropped us off at the honeymoon suite—which was actually another luxury villa—in a golf cart.

"Do you want me to have breakfast delivered in the morning?" he asked. "Shall I book you some spa treatments?"

"Breakfast would be good, but I want to visit my parents tomorrow."

We'd shared a tearful phone call earlier, but Dad heard the laughter in the background and told me to go back to my friends and enjoy myself. Tomorrow, I wanted to talk to him properly, and I longed for a hug from my mum.

"What time? I'll arrange a car."

I'd really miss Akeem when we left. "Mid-morning? About ten?"

"It'll be waiting by the lobby. Unless you want to borrow the Mustang again?"

"Emmy's back now."

"So?"

"Won't *she* want to drive it?"

"There are three certainties in life—death, taxes,

and the fact that Emmy won't get out of bed before noon tomorrow. I'll bring the key over in the morning."

The morning... I needed to speak to Chloe too, but I had a lot of bridges to mend there. Mum told me she'd got married and had a baby, and I'd missed everything. We'd always sworn that if either of us got married, the other would be maid of honour, but instead of helping with her wedding preparations, I'd disappeared. I knew we'd never be close again, accepted it, but I hoped that if I apologised, we could at least stay friends.

But I'd think about all that in the morning. Tonight, I just needed to sleep.

Which came with its own challenges.

"Are you okay to share the bed?" I asked Russell. "What if I bump into you?"

"If you think you're taking the sofa, you've got another think coming."

"But I don't want to hurt you."

"I've got morphine, and I'll take my chances. I'm just sorry I can't make love to you. You've got no idea how much I want to."

I eyed up the bulge in his trousers. "Oh, I think I do."

He saw where I was looking and gave me a wonky smile. "You have that effect on me."

"Perhaps I could give it a suck?"

"I can't even breathe hard at the moment without it hurting."

"Sorry."

"Don't apologise for that man. Brenner's out of both of our lives now, and that's where he's staying."

"I'll take the left side of the bed, shall I?" Since the bullet went into his right lung.

"I think that would be best."

That night, I slept soundly for the first time in over three years, listening to Russell's breathing in the dark until I drifted off. Holding hands while we slept wasn't exactly what I'd had in mind for when I found the man of my dreams, but it would do until he healed. Then we'd have to make up for lost time.

We'd have the rest of our lives together, and thanks to him believing in me, I was free.

Free to travel.

Free to smile.

Free to love.

Free to do whatever the hell I wanted.

"Don't hug him, Mum!"

I managed to stop her just before she flung her arms around Russell, and he bent his knees and managed to kiss her on the cheek instead. Then I got the hug I'd been craving as she squashed the breath out of me.

"I thought we'd never see you again," she said, tears streaming down her cheeks. Now do you see where I got it from? "We understood why you had to leave, but that didn't make it any easier."

"I just want to forget the last three years ever happened, apart from meeting Russell, of course. And Tai, and Ren, and all the people from Blackwood."

"I don't even know who Tai and Ren are, dear. You'll have to tell us the whole story over tea. Your dad's put the kettle on."

Dad hugged me too and settled for a reserved

handshake with Russell. He'd always been a man of few words.

"And Chloe's coming over. We thought you'd want to see her."

"How upset is she?"

"Well, I can't pretend she was overjoyed that you upped and left without a word, but she realises you didn't have a lot of choice under the circumstances. Plus you also inspired her new business venture, so she's grateful for that. Oh, here she is now."

She had a new car, a minivan with a kiddie seat in the back, but she looked exactly the same. Wavy blonde hair, freckles from the sun, and a floaty, flowery dress. She made most of her clothes herself.

"Kylie!" She ran over and gave Mum competition in the hugging stakes. "You look amazing. All the time you were gone, I kept imagining you starving in some flea pit, but wow." Then she turned to Russell. "Is this the guy who got shot?"

Russell mustered up a smile. "The one and only."

"Russell, this is my friend Chloe. Don't listen to any of the stories she tells about me. Chloe, this is Russell. He's...he's..." What did I call him? We hadn't put a label on our relationship yet. "He's my everything."

"Aw, that's so sweet! And she only doesn't want me to tell the stories because they're true."

"I like her," Russell whispered to me as we walked into the house. "I can't wait to hear these stories."

"We might have to leave early."

"What was that?" Mum asked. "Leave early? You don't want to do that. Remember the last time you wanted to leave a get-together early? You tried to climb out of Uncle Bert's bathroom window and fell into the toilet."

Chloe turned and grinned. "My stories are better."

This was going to be a really long day, wasn't it? But I'd still love every minute of it, and the relief that Chloe wasn't mad at me was indescribable. I had my life back.

Inside, Mum and Dad's little terrier, Benjy, bounced around our feet, yipping and yapping. He'd always had more energy than manners, and any attempts to train him had failed miserably. He knocked Chloe's handbag onto the floor and scratched my leg, but I couldn't even be mad.

"Hey," I said half-heartedly. "Sit. Stay."

Of course, he completely ignored me, and I bent to help Chloe pick up her things. She always carried enough stuff for an impromptu weekend away, and Benjy grabbed a tiny doll from the pile and ran off down the hallway.

"Give that back!" I yelled after him. This was just like the old days, other than Russell's quiet chuckle behind me.

"Oh, it doesn't matter," Chloe said. "It was a gift for you, but you probably don't need it anymore since Michael's dead now."

I finally managed to lever Benjy's jaws open and retrieve the... "What *is* this?"

It looked like a tiny doll, but it had Michael's freaking face. Yuck! I threw it back to Benjy so he could do his worst.

"It's a personalised voodoo doll. I've started selling them in my Etsy store, and they're really popular."

"*This* is your new business venture?"

"Your mum told you? Yes, people send me their hated ones' photos, and I make the dolls at home while

Sophie's sleeping."

Totally tasteless, but who cared? At least somebody was benefitting from the tragedy.

"Is Benjy eating another Michael doll?" Mum asked, coming back with a plate of biscuits. "I like to think he did his bit to help. And with those other two arseholes as well."

"Mum!" I'd never heard her use that sort of language before. Seemed I wasn't the only person Michael had changed.

"The dog's got a bit of work left to do with Owen," Russell said. "He's still alive."

"No, he died in the hospital this morning, that's what the news said. Custard cream?"

Owen was gone? It was really over?

Russell checked his phone, and a smile spread across his face. "It's true. Complications from his gunshot wound, apparently."

"Good riddance." The last bit of tension ebbed out of me.

"Indeed." Russell turned back to my mum, and she beamed at him. "I'd love a custard cream. Thanks very much, Mrs. Nichols."

With the family reunion complete, it was time to look to the future when we got back to the resort. We couldn't stay there forever, although Akeem had booked us the honeymoon suite for the rest of the week.

Russell had swapped his laptop for an iPad, and he lay outside in the shade, staring up at it.

"Working again?"

"Nope. I'm taking the week off. My staff think I've gone mad."

The sun lounger was made for two, so I snuggled up next to him. "Houses? You're looking at houses."

"Yup. Glad I didn't buy that place in Morocco now. What's Indooroopilly like? I'm not even sure if I've pronounced that right."

"You're buying a house in *Brisbane*?"

"It's more cost-effective than renting in the long run."

"But your company's in London."

"Yes, but you're not, and I want to spend as much time as possible with you. Phone sex just isn't the same."

"Who says we have to live in Brisbane?"

"Well, I just assumed..."

"Mr. Weisz, which part of 'I don't care where I go as long as I'm with you' did you not understand? I'll come to London. Yes, I'll still need to visit my parents and Chloe, but I've got no career and no home to keep me here. It's time for a fresh start, and my life's with you."

"Are you serious?"

"I can work anywhere. Graphic design isn't that lucrative, but I can pay a bit towards an apartment, and —"

He kissed me before I could finish. "I love you. And I paid off the mortgage on my London apartment with my first bonus." Wow, twice over. "Plus you're not exactly on the breadline."

"Actually, I am. Last time I checked, my bank account had minus three hundred dollars in it."

"Uh..."

He had that shifty look, the one where he didn't want to tell me something, but there was no need. Didn't he understand nothing would ever be as bad as the blowjob video?

"Russell, what is it?"

"Right before Brenner arrived at the villa, I might have moved his nest egg."

"You *what*?"

"I figured if I waited, he'd move it himself."

"You stole Michael's money?"

"How about we go with 'acquired'?"

"Okay, acquired. How much are we talking?"

"Roughly four million dollars. US dollars, not Australian—it looked as if he was getting ready to run abroad."

Holy shit. "We can't just keep it! I mean, it's the proceeds of crime. We'll be arrested."

"No, we won't. I've bounced it around a bit, and the police won't find it now. Think of it as restitution. He took three years of your life, Kylie, and you can't get that back. I'd say you're owed something for what he did, wouldn't you?"

Four million dollars? That was a hell of a lot of money. Yes, Michael had wrecked my career and forced me to leave my home, but did the years I'd spent on the run really count as me earning it?

"Keeping it still feels wrong."

"You'd rather give it to the police? After *their* part in this?"

"Well, no, but—"

"Donate it to charity if you'd prefer, but the government has got quite enough money already."

I thought about it, and Russell gave me the space to

do so. Michael had made me lose everything. My home, my job, everything I'd worked for. He'd tried to end my life, and he'd nearly succeeded in taking Russell's. And my former colleagues? They'd abandoned me too. Screw them. If we turned the cash in, they'd probably spend it on new office furniture or something.

"I think I'll give part of it to Hanna." She'd been living in fear too.

"And the rest?"

A smile twitched at my lips. "We should take an actual holiday. One where I don't have to kill anyone."

"I'm on board with that. And then what?"

"Then it looks like I need to learn how to ride the Tube and hail black cabs. And sort out a visa."

"A visa?" Emmy's voice came from behind us. I hadn't even heard her approach. "Where are you going? Sorry for sneaking up, but I figured you wouldn't be doing the nasty since Russell still can't breathe properly."

"Uh, London. I'm going to move to London with Russell."

"Awesome. Let me know if there's any problems with the paperwork, and I'll pull some strings. Do you need a job? I'd offer Russell one, but he already makes bank."

A job? "What kind of a job?"

"Entry-level investigator? I saw your record. You were a good cop before you fell in with the wrong crowd."

I echoed Russell. "Are you serious? I screwed up my *own case*."

"You were trying to solve it with both hands tied behind your back. Go back a few years before Michael brainwashed you, and you had the right instincts. So yes, I'm serious."

Wow. A real job offer. Doing something I actually enjoyed. Tempting, but I wanted a couple of months to adjust to the new normal first. And maybe I'd offer my spare time to a charity. Pay it forward now that I had the cushion of Michael's money to fall back on.

"Can I think about it? I was considering doing some volunteer work for a while."

"Sure. Just call me whenever. I also have a charity foundation in London if you feel like helping out."

"What kind of charity foundation?"

"We help teenagers who didn't have the best start to find their places in life."

Helping people to find their place... That sounded like something I could get involved with. Spending three years on the run had taught me the value of being able to put down roots.

Then Russell spoke. "Emmy, about that job..."

I'd never seen her look truly surprised before. "For *you*?"

"Luke mentioned he did some consultancy for Blackwood. These last few weeks, I've learned that it *is* possible to delegate without the entire company falling apart, and I plan to do that more in the future. And I enjoyed the investigative work. The thrill of the chase, if you like."

"And you want to consult?"

"I'm available if you ever need me. After what you did for Tai in Egypt and Kylie here, a few hours of my time is the least I owe you."

Emmy grinned. "I might just take you up on that. Did you have any more thoughts on the future of

Ether?"

"I've given it a lot of consideration, and I've decided not to pull the plug. For now. For all the bad it does, it does good too. Mimi told me she knows of a number of battered women who used it to escape from abusive relationships, and I don't want to remove that safety net. But Kaito Nakamura will make it known that he'll assist the authorities should someone use the app to break the law."

"I think that's a happy medium."

"Leyton mentioned he had cases where access to Ether might be useful, so we can start there."

Emmy grinned at him. "Sounds good to me. Well, it looks like I'll see you both in London, then."

"You're leaving?" I asked.

"Me and Mimi are going on a trip."

Rather her than me. A holiday with Mimi would be like a stay in purgatory with added suffering. "Somewhere nice?"

"Indonesia. Sun, scuba diving, the best satay chicken, and who can forget Sijahtra coffee? Oh, and we need to see a bug-eyed drug dealer about a funeral."

"I'm going to pretend I didn't hear that last part, okay?"

"Don't worry; we'll make it look like an accident. Anyhow, I just came over to invite you to the grand opening of the New Egypt Museum. We don't have a date yet, but the money seized from a certain Deputy Minister of Antiquities has been earmarked for the build."

"The Deputy Minister of Antiquities? Is that to do with the smuggling case?"

"Yup. There's still the odd loose end to tie up, but

they got him. Turned out he'd been using his ill-gotten gains to fund his lifestyle, and now neither of his wives are happy with him."

"Two wives? Tell me they knew about each other."

"Nope. One of them got arrested for assault after she allegedly whacked him over his head with a cucumber, but the other one gave her an alibi so they had to let her go. So, the museum thing?"

I was still processing the cucumber thing. At least it hadn't been a bronze statue, or she might have needed more than a fake alibi.

"We'd love to come to the party," Russell said. "Wouldn't we, darling?"

Did I really want to return to Egypt? With Russell by my side, I did. Our first invite as a couple, and it promised to be spectacular.

"Yes, we would."

The end. Or is it the beginning?
Would you like to hear more from Mimi and Rix?
Let me know...

What's next?

My next book will be *Glitter*, a novella that slots in after Ultraviolet in the Blackwood Security series, releasing at the end of 2019.

Glitter

At thirty-two years old, Ana Petrova's had enough of death. She never wanted to be an assassin anyway. With a young daughter now the centre of her world, Ana's determined to settle into her new life in Virginia and do whatever it is suburban moms do.

But her friend Emmy has other ideas. A trip to New York proves that even the brightest places can have dark shadows, and Ana's forced to consider whether there might still be a need for her skills after all.

For more details: www.elise-noble.com/glitter

The next book in the Blackwood Elements series will be Nickel, releasing in 2020.

Nickel

When Sloane Mullins catches her boyfriend in a compromising position with another woman, her meddling friend Leah decides that a better model is exactly what Sloane needs, whether she wants to start dating again or not.

Meanwhile, colleague Logan steps in to rescue her from one disaster after another. What if the perfect man has been under her nose the whole time?

For more details: www.elise-noble.com/nickel

If you enjoyed Bronze, please consider leaving a review.

For an author, every review is incredibly important. Not only do they make us feel warm and fuzzy inside, readers consider them when making their decision whether or not to buy a book. Even a line saying you enjoyed the book or what your favourite part was helps a lot.

WANT TO STALK ME?

For updates on my new releases, giveaways, and other random stuff, you can sign up for my newsletter on my website:
www.elise-noble.com

Facebook:
www.facebook.com/EliseNobleAuthor

Twitter: @EliseANoble

Instagram: @elise_noble

If you're on Facebook, you may also like to join Team Blackwood for exclusive giveaways, sneak previews, and book-related chat. Be the first to find out about new stories, and you might even see your name or one of your ideas make it into print!

And if you'd like to read my books for FREE, you can also find details of how to join my review team.

Would you like to join Team Blackwood?

www.elise-noble.com/team-blackwood

END OF BOOK STUFF

Russell and Kylie both came out of a novel I serialised in my newsletter last year, then called Untitled (because I had no idea where the story was heading or what it was going to be about, lol), and now published as Copper. Copper stars Tai, an English girl who did something I suspect we've all dreamed about from time to time—she walked out of her life in search of a new adventure. About halfway through, I asked my readers which of the two men they wanted Tai to end up with, but what I didn't tell them (sorry!) was that I planned for whoever they didn't pick to end up with Kylie.

And so we have Bronze. Originally, I figured I'd wrap up Kylie's story in the epilogue, then I realised there was actually quite a lot involved, so I figured, hey, maybe a novella, but that didn't work out either. Part of that was Mimi's fault. I honestly don't know where she came from, but I like her. Maybe she'll be back? Who knows...

The fact that this was meant to be a novella led to the title. Yes, I know Bronze isn't an element, but since it was meant to be book 7.5, I figured it would be cute to use an alloy instead. Then I ballsed-up the length, but by that point, the title was stuck in my head. Ho hum.

I'm planning to sneak in one more book before the

end of the year—I was missing Emmy, Ana and Bradley, so I wrote them a little novella that slots in after Ultraviolet. But since this will be my last book before Christmas, I'd like to take the opportunity to say Merry Christmas if you celebrate it, and Happy Holidays if you don't. I hope you have a lovely December.

Elise

Other books by Elise Noble

The Blackwood Security Series
For the Love of Animals (Nate & Carmen - prequel)
Black is my Heart (prequel)
Pitch Black
Into the Black
Forever Black
Gold Rush
Gray is my Heart
Neon (novella)
Out of the Blue
Ultraviolet
Glitter (novella) (2019)
Red Alert
White Hot
The Scarlet Affair
Quicksilver
The Girl with the Emerald Ring (2020)
Red After Dark (2020)
When the Shadows Fall (2020)

The Blackwood Elements Series
Oxygen
Lithium
Carbon
Rhodium

Platinum
Lead
Copper
Bronze
Nickel (2020)

The Blackwood UK Series
Joker in the Pack
Cherry on Top (novella)
Roses are Dead
Shallow Graves
Indigo Rain
Pass the Parcel (TBA)

Blackwood Casefiles
Stolen Hearts

Blackstone House
Hard Lines (TBA)
Hard Tide (TBA)

The Electi Series
Cursed
Spooked
Possessed
Demented (2020)

The Trouble Series
Trouble in Paradise
Nothing but Trouble
24 Hours of Trouble

Standalone

Life
Twisted (short stories)
A Very Happy Christmas (novella)

Printed in Great Britain
by Amazon